A Novel By
Kween Pen

Acknowledgments

As always, I must begin by giving God all of the glory and honor He truly deserves. Lord, I thank you for everything you have done, are doing, and will do in the future. Without you, none of this would be possible. I thank you for the multitude of blessings and the incredible favor over my life. After everything I've been through, Lord, I know you must have a higher purpose for me.

It's a requirement that I thank my two little rugrats, Aniya and Antoine Jr., for doing nothing more than being yourselves. The smiles, the hugs, the kisses all make my day as a parent and give me reason to just keep going no matter what obstacles may come my way.

To my team! Where would I be without my team? To Mr. Willie J. LeBlanc; my editor, graphic designer (cover art), format specialist, and avid reader: thank you for everything. Once again, you've waved your wand over this book and worked your magic. To the baddest promoter in the land: a huge thank you yo Authoress Crystal Alexis for all that you do. To my dedicated test readers: Danielle Holley (who doubles as my best friend), L'Vetrious Davis (who doubles as my partner in crime), and Amy Tassin, thank you for being patient with me and always giving me your honest opinions. Even when I send you unfinished work, half of a book, or just a teaser, I can always depend on you three for the 100% truth.

Where there is love lost, there will be love found. A huge thank you to everyone who didn't believe in me, hated on me, did me wrong, stabbed me in the back, lied on me, used me, abused me, or doubted me. Everything you did taught me very important lessons and made me that much stronger and wiser.

And to that one special person who created the monster I am today and then stuck around to deal with my aftermath, where would I be without you? You push me to always be my best self, reach for the furthest star, and keep my head held high. As incredible as you believe me to be, I owe it all to you, as you are equally amazing. Thank you for just being you. You know who you are.

To my readers: to my incredible group of dedicated and loyal readers, especially my book hoarding cousins, T, Cort, Sinora, and Sabrina, I thank you all for taking this journey with me and being along for the ride. To my new readers: welcome to my world. I hope you stick around a while. To you all: The wheels haven't fallen off, so we're going to keep rocking. Thank you for your continued support!

Chapter 1

Volleyball. Rugby. Croquet. Chemistry. Biology. Ballet. Calculus. Trigonometry. I sat staring at the clock perched on the wall above the dry erase board. Fifteen more minutes to endure and then I'd be free to enjoy a summer of swimming, slumber partying, and sleeping in. There were no lectures on the last day of school before summer break. The teachers had no lesson plans and there were no homework assignments to take up or write down. We weren't paying any attention to the teacher, and she wasn't paying any attention to us. This was obvious given that Brian's hand was up Madison's skirt and Tristian was rolling a blunt underneath his desk.

"Pst… Hey! Bre'ana!" Tristian whispered to me. I already knew what he wanted and he already knew what my response would be. Tristian just enjoyed fucking with me for no reason.

"What?!" I whispered back with an attitude all over my face.

"You wanna smoke this blunt with me after class? It's Kush," he offered as if it was an irresistible temptation.

"Tristian, how many times do I have to tell you? I'm straight on that shit. I don't smoke."

"I'll get you to smoke with me one day," he told me. "You should lighten up a little bit, Bre. It's summer break."

"If I smoke that mess I won't be able to pass my drug tests, which means I'll get kicked off of all of the teams and lost my chances at getting sports scholarships."

"It's the summer, Bre. You don't have to worry about randoms for the next two months."

"I'm good, Tris," I told him as I rolled my eyes and went back to the chemical equations I had been doing before I looked up at the clock. My chemistry teacher, Mr. Greer, had allowed me to keep my chemistry textbook for the summer to practice as long as I agreed to bring it back in the same condition the next fall.

I had a true talent in balancing chemical equations, and I had plans to become a chemical engineer. I had the periodic table completely memorized, including atomic masses, by the time I was ten. I could break down any combination of elements into protons and neutrons faster than Tristian could break down weed to fill a cigar.

As opposite as I knew we were, Tristian still had had a crush on me since we met when we were six. We had been in the same classes every year since the first grade. Tristian always sat one seat behind me, one row to my right no matter what class we were in, no matter how close to the front I sat. His seat in every class was always determined by mine.

As a child, it was cute but annoying. Over the years, though, I had gotten used to it and even became more considerate of him. But somewhere along the way, Tristian had gotten introduced to marijuana, and it was at that point that any question I had ever had about whether or not he may possibly be a decent option for a boyfriend had been answered.

My parents were prominent members of Memphis society. My father was Dr. Gerald Braxton, Ph. D. He was an OB/GYN and owned ten practices in Memphis and the surrounding areas, including several ultrasound and x-ray clinics. He was the go-to doctor for every woman in any upper-class social circle in the city. My mother was a criminal court prosecutor for the state. She had been the lead prosecutor on twenty-nine murder cases, and she had won all of them but two. She was prosecutor Brenda Braxton and everyone in any corner or crevice of the legal system knew her name. I had seen grown men cringe when they found out she was the prosecutor on their cases.

My parents both worked long hours and made an ungodly amount of money. I was showered with high-priced gifts and I attended the best co-ed private school money could buy in our city. My grades were always exceptional and I excelled in every sport, every instrument, every hobby that I ever set my mind to try. I had a line of trophies on my bedroom wall from spelling bees, science fairs, ballet recitals, rugby tournaments, volleyball championships, and so many other endeavors.

Tristian had had the same upbringing. His father was a famous defense attorney and his mother was a heart surgeon. Unlike me, Tristian was not an only child. He had a younger brother named Kyle who was six years younger than us. His family lived two streets over from mine, and he and I would walk to each other's houses as preteens to study for tests and help each other with homework. I'm sure both of our parents expected us to end up together eventually. I just couldn't see myself with Tristian.

The bell rang. I closed my paper inside of the textbook and slid it into my backpack before tossing it on my back. I smiled widely as I came face- to- face with my best friend, Chloe, as I walked into the hallway.

"Finally free!" she exhaled.

"I know, right!" I laughed. "We're officially juniors now!" I told her.

"Girl, I don't care what we are as long as we're away from this damn school for the next two months!" she yelled as we maneuvered through the crowded hallway full of students rushing to get as far away from the building as quickly as possible. I laughed at her as she popped a Blow Pop between her "Blushing Bride" red painted lips. "When are you leaving?"

"Monday morning," I told her. "You wanna come over tonight? You can help me finish packing and then we can watch old horror movies and eat pizza."

"I can't. I told Brad I'd go out with him tonight," she declined.

"Brad? When did this happen?"

"A couple of days ago in Fisher's English class," she told me. "He slipped me a not with the 'check yes or no' boxes," she laughed.

"Just stupid!" I laughed with her. "It's cool, though. I'll catch up with you before I leave," I told her as I opened the door to my Infiniti QX80 my parents had just given me for my last birthday, an upgrade from the Honda Accord I used to drive.

"Okay," Chloe yelled over the roof of her Buick Lacrosse. "See you later."

When I made it home, the house was empty as usual. Both of my parents were still at their respective offices, so I was left to entertain myself. I popped my earbuds in as I opened the fridge and grabbed the Snapple I had left inside to chill before I left for school. I made myself a turkey sandwich and went upstairs to my room.

I had two more days in Memphis before I headed down to Ansley, Georgia, Atlanta's beautiful suburb full of incredibly architected residences to spend the summer with my aunt Sharon and my cousin Shaniece whose birthday was two days after mine. Shaniece and I could have been sisters. We were inseparable every time we got together and required almost no supervision because we never got into anything. We'd spend half of the summer at the mall and the other half at the pool and be in tears when the summer came to an end and I had to return home.

I sat on my bed looking around my room as I ate my turkey sandwich. Though it wasn't in complete disarray, I knew I had to finish packing so that I could clean up before I left for the summer. I sorted through the shopping bags and packages that had come in the mail, choosing which dresses, shorts, and crop tops would make it into my Louis Vuitton suitcase. I never packed much, and I always returned from Georgia with more luggage than I had come with.

My mom was the first to make it home, bursting into the house with her normal Friday routine of dropping her keys and two large pizzas on the kitchen counter, yelling my name up the stairs, and then going straight into her room to get out of her suit. My dad made his entrance an hour later, following his own routine. He dropped his keys next to my mom's, grabbed a slice of pizza which he inhaled on his way up the stairs, and knocked on my door. When I opened it, he took my face in both hands and kissed me on the forehead. I was his angel and he was my superhero. He kept up with everything I did at school, made sure to be at every championship game, and had been in the front row when I won each and every one of my trophies. Until I had started driving, my mom had been responsible for getting me back and forth from practices and rehearsals. We were the perfect little family. The successful doctor, the powerhouse attorney, and an overachiever as a daughter. They were the perfect couple and I was the perfect result. I had a promising future that was leading down the road to me becoming a brilliant chemical engineer. I had it all.

Chapter 2

I could tell by Aunt Sharon's face when I pulled into the driveway that she would likely kill my mother the next time they saw each other. Shaniece stood next to her gawking at my new truck as I parked behind her silver Lexus LS and got out.

"Breeeeeee!!!" she squealed as she ran up to me and threw her arms around my neck. "I missed you so much!"

"I missed you too," I said, smiling widely, happy to see my cousin again.

"Hey, Auntie," I said as I hugged her.

"Where are your bags? C'mon. Let's get you inside before this poor child suffocates you," she told me.

"I've got so much to tell you," Shaniece said as we walked up the stairs to her bedroom.

"Me too," I agreed.

"No," she said as she gave me the eye, "I've got a lot to tell you."

"Well, okay then," I giggled. "Where's the popcorn?"

"Believe me, you're going to need a movie theater bucket for all of the shit I'm about to tell you," she said as she opened the door of the spare bedroom for me to bring my bags inside.

"You've got that much going on?" I looked at her with a raised eyebrow.

"Girl, if you only knew," she said.

"Well, tell me. Here, help me put my clothes in the closet and dresser while you tell me what's been up with you," I told her as I handed her one of my suitcases.

"So you remember I was telling you about David last time we talked?" she asked as she unzipped the bag.

"Yeah, but you two weren't serious or anything when you were telling me about him," I said as I put a stack of shorts in a dresser drawer.

"Bre, we're sixteen. Nothing is serious," she laughed.

"And yet, everything is serious," I contradicted her jokingly.

"Isn't it, though?" she laughed.

"So what's up with him? What happened?"

"So… we went to the movies together a couple of weeks ago, and we sat all the way at the back of the movie theater because we went in the middle of the day on a Sunday, so you know the movie theater was hella empty."

"Of course."

"You have PINK panties? And bras?" she interrupted herself.

"Yeah, I just use my mom's Victoria's Secret card. I've got plenty of PINK stuff," I told her.

"Well, damn. So anyway," she continued, "we were in the back of the theater watching the movie, and he leaned over and wrapped his arm around me. So I snuggled beneath him and he lifted my chin and kissed me."

"You kissed David?" I asked her.

"Yep."

"But wasn't that awkward? I mean, you've known him almost all your life. Wasn't it weird?"

"Not really because he's a great kisser."

"In comparison to what? He's the only person you've ever kissed. He may not actually be that good of a kisser. He's just all you know."

"I've kissed plenty of other guys," she said indignantly.

"You're such a liar! No, you haven't!"

"Yes, I have," she insisted. "David's like the fifth guy I've kissed."

"You never told me any of this," I frowned at her.

"It must've slipped my mind I guess," she said as she shrugged her shoulders.

"So your first kiss slipped your mind? You lying heifer! You're full of shit! Who'd you kiss?"

"A couple of boys from school. You don't know them," she said nonchalantly.

"Well damn. So if you've kissed a bunch of guys...."

"I didn't say I kissed a bunch of guys," she interrupted me. "I said four or five."

"Okay, so if you've kissed four guys before him, then what's so special about him?" I asked her. "I mean, it was just another kiss."

"I mean, yeah, it was just another kiss, but if you let me finish…"

"Well, go ahead," I giggled as I closed a drawer and plopped down on the bed.

"Okay, so we're kissing and shit and nobody is paying us any attention because we're on the back row. He slipped his hand up my skirt, and I was all nervous and stuff because you know I've never gone that far with anybody. I had on a thong because I didn't want any panty lines in my cute little Polo skirt. So he was rubbing back and forth over my thong, and it felt so damn good," she said as she rolled her eyes into the back of her head for emphasis. Typical Shaniece. She was always so overly dramatic.

"Wow," I said.

"That's not it though. So he was rubbing back and forth, and I decided to follow his lead. I unzipped his jeans and slipped my hand inside," she said with a smirk.

"Oh shit! You rubbed his dick? Was it big?"

"I didn't just rub it. I stroked it, and yes, it was… I mean, I honestly didn't have anything to compare it to, but it didn't seem small at all," she giggled.

"Damn, Shaniece," I mumbled. I didn't know what to say. I guess I really had missed some things.

"So that still ain't all," she said.

"What?" I laughed nervously, afraid of what she was possibly going to say next.

"Yeah, girl. So I'm rubbing on him and he was rock hard. So he pushed my thong to the side and slipped his fingers inside of me," she revealed.

"You're lying!" I whispered in disbelief.

"I promise!"

"He fingered you?"

"Yes!"

"What did it feel like?"

"It's hard to explain. It was like he touched a spot that had been dying to be touched. He scratched an itch I couldn't reach. I can't explain it, but it felt so good," she said.

"Damn, Shaniece!"

"I know, right!" she laughed.

"So what happened after y'all left the movie theater?"

"He took me home and we made out in the car before I went inside," she said nonchalantly.

"But, I mean, are y'all dating now? I mean, y'all are to-gether, right?" I asked.

"Oh, yeah, yeah. We're dating now. That's bae," she said as she smiled proudly.

"Look at you! Doing grown woman shit now. I'm slick jealous. I haven't done any of that," I admitted.

"I know. You would've told me if you did."

"Yeah, so why didn't you tell me?" I asked as I leaned against the dresser.

"I don't know. I guess I was waiting until you came down here, but I think I didn't want you to be mad at me either," she said.

"Mad at you? Why would I be mad at you?" I frowned.

"Because you haven't done any of that yet," she stated.

"True, but I can't be mad at you just because you have," I told her as I played with my nails. "I haven't had time for guys anyway. I'm always so busy with everything else. I guess one day I'll meet somebody I like and eventually it'll go there," I assured her.

"Yeah, well, I'm always busy too. Between all of the homework from my AP classes, cheerleading, and plus I started gymnastics a few months ago, I hardly have any time to do anything other than sleep."

"Obviously you've got some kind of spare time. You found time to go on a date with David," I told her.

"I'll always have time for David," she giggled.

"Yeah, well, you just be careful. You know our parents want us to believe we can get pregnant from kissing," I reminded her.

"Ha! Girl please!" she laughed.

"Well, I'm about to hop in the shower. It's been a long drive. I'll probably go ahead and call it a night."

"This early? You just got here," she whined.

"I know, but I'm tired. Plus we've got the whole summer. You'll be tired of seeing me by the time I leave to go back home."

"Never!" she said as she shook her head. "I always hate it when you leave to go back home."

"Me too," I agreed.

"Well, good night," she said as she went to the door. "See you in the morning."

I tried not to feel some type of way about what Shaniece had told me. Honestly, I was happy for my cousin. I certainly wasn't mad at her like she thought I would be. But deep inside, I was jealous. I had always been so focused on school, sports, and everything else I had going on that I had completely skipped the boy crazy phase all of my friends had been experiencing.

Shaniece is my little cousin, I thought to myself in the shower. I should be ahead of her. I wasn't ready for sex and I knew it. Just the thought of it still scared me to death. I couldn't understand how Shaniece had gotten comfortable enough with David to allow him to do all of those things to her, kiss her so deeply, touch her in those places. I had never felt that comfortable with any guy, not even Tristian.

I wondered what I felt like as I laid in bed that night with Shaniece's story still heavy on my mind. What did it feel like to like a guy or to have feelings for one? What did it feel like having someone's lips pressed passionately against yours or his tongue in your mouth? I couldn't imagine what it felt like to have a guy slip his fingers between my legs and caress me there. I couldn't imagine any of it but wanted to know for myself.

Chapter 3

Shaniece and I spent most of the next few days in and around the pool in their backyard. I listened as Shaniece told me all about David and the things they talked about, and I watched enviously as she texted him endlessly all day. David was Shaniece's first boyfriend, and I could tell she was falling for him hard. They would talk on the phone for hours at night and it seemed their conversations never ran dry.

While Shaniece was preoccupied with her phone conversations with David, I kept my head buried in my chemistry book, completing countless exercises and equations. When I wasn't feeling the chemistry book, I whipped out my iPad and did biology research. When all else failed, I worked on calculus and trigonometry equations.

I sat watching Shaniece as we lounged by the pool one day. She was on the phone with David, as usual, and I had just gotten out of the pool and was lying across a chair. I noticed the change in my cousin as she talked. Her demeanor had changed. Her posture was different. Her smile was wider. Her already beautifully mocha-kissed skin had a glow. She had a smile in her eyes, and I could even hear her smile in her voice. So this is what a man does for a woman? I asked myself. He makes her happy. He makes her complete, I told myself.

I trusted Shaniece's word. She and David hadn't gone all

the way yet, but I could tell her curiosity was piqued. I could read her thoughts sometimes. I knew what I would have been thinking if I was Shaniece. If his fingers inside of me felt that good, what would it feel like if he put his dick in? She never said it specifically or directly, but I could tell they had been talking about it.

"Bre, you wanna go to a party with me?" she asked as I was coming out of the bathroom one day.

"A party? Sure. What kind of party?"

"It's a house party my friend is throwing. Her parents are out of town for two weeks, so she's inviting a bunch of us from school," she explained.

"I don't know. I mean, I don't know any of the kids that you go to school with, and she probably won't want people she doesn't know there."

"I'm sure she won't care. I know other people will bring people with them too," she assured me.

"Well, if you're sure it's okay, I'll go."

"Cool! Get ready. We'll leave around eight."

I went through every drawer and looked at every dress twice. Nothing seemed just right. I finally decided on a peach off the shoulder crop top and a pair of white high waisted shorts. I pulled my hair into a neat donut and left some hair hanging in my face for bangs. I did my makeup and added some large gold hoops, gold bangles, and a gold chain belt and blew kisses at myself in the mirror.

Shaniece opened her bedroom door clad in a navy blue and white crop top and navy blue tennis skirt, her makeup flawless, her hair precisely curled. Still, she had the nerve to be standing there with an unsure look on her face. Shaniece and I looked too much alike for me to allow her to doubt herself. If she wasn't cute, then neither was I. She was bright-skinned with freckles and I was mocha. We were both five-foot- four. She was a hundred twenty-five pounds, and I was one fifteen. I kept my hair long and she kept hers neatly cut at a medium length. We had the same taste in clothing and shoes, the same emotions and attitudes, the same facial structure and expressions. People who didn't know us thought we were twins.

"I like it," I said as I grinned widely at her.

"You sure? I couldn't find anything that I just felt good about," she said.

"You look great," I assured her. "Is David going to be there?" I asked as she checked her hair in the mirror.

"Yep. I'm glad you're finally going to meet him."

"It'll be nice to put a face with the name," I told her.

"That's true. You ready? Let's roll!"

*   ~   *   ~   *

Aunt Sharon had no clue where we were, and I was sure if

she found out she would murder us on the spot. I had driven my Infiniti all the way across town to a neighborhood I had never even heard of under the turn by turn directions Shaniece was giving me. When we made it into the gritty inner city, I knew that Shaniece had lied about something because there was no way she was friends with someone from this part of town. The deeper we got into the city, the more suspicious looking characters we passed, the more uncomfortable I became, and the more questions that wrote themselves on the list in my head.

It turned out that it was a party of a friend of a friend of a friend of Shaniece, and she had found out about the party from a homemade flyer and a few whispers in the hallway at school. I could tell, however, that Shaniece had no idea what she was getting the two of us into. That became even more obvious when I turned onto the street where the party was supposed to be taking place. I had never been to the projects; I had only heard about them. When we turned into the apartment complex with no grass, a rundown playground with broken glass shattered across it, a parking lot full of flattened tires on vehicles that looked like they were or should have been inoperable, rats the size of house cats walking calmly between the buildings, and t-shirts, bras, panties, boxers, and nursing scrubs hanging from lines at the back doors of the apartments, I knew for sure that Shaniece had lost her damn mind.

We had started hearing the thud of the bass a mile before we approached the complex. When we pulled up, the music was nearly deafening. Teenagers were standing outside with forty ounce beers in their hands. The girls were all holding red Solo cups. I looked at Shaniece like she had grown three

19

more heads.

"C'mon, Bre," she whined. "It'll be fun."

"I hardly call being murdered fun, Shaniece. Do you know any of these people?"

"Ugh! You won't die! And I'm sure anybody I know is inside, not standing outside like some bums," she assured me. "Plus part of the fun is that no one knows you, so you're free to be whoever you want to be and do whatever you want to do, and nobody you know is there to judge you or remind you of any of the mistakes you made."

"Mistakes?" I scoffed. "I'm not trying to do anything at all up in there, let alone make any kind of damn mistakes," I told her.

"C'mon, Bre. Let's just stay a little while. We already drove across town to get here. We might as well see what's up," she said and nodded in the direction of the apartment with the red light and music playing.

"Niecey, this shit doesn't look safe at all," I told her.

"No house party is safe, Bre. You always run the risk of the neighbors calling the cops or some stupid guys getting into a fight or shooting up the place. If we wanted to be safe, we would've stayed at home, ordered pizza or Chinese, and sat up watching "The Notebook" and doing each other's hair. I didn't come here to be safe. I came here to have fun. Now c'mon," she said and then flung the door open and hopped out.

20

I had no choice but to follow her because I certainly wasn't going to allow her to go inside alone. I knew I was entering the unknown and possibly a realm of hell I had never seen, but we had come together and we would leave together. I followed Shaniece into the cloud of marijuana and cigarette smoke that the entire apartment was under, trying to stay aware of my surroundings.

"Bre, come here! I want you to meet David!" she yelled over the music. "David, this is my cousin Bre'ana. She's from Memphis. Bre, this is my boyfriend David," she introduced us.

"It's nice to meet you," David said as he offered his hand for me to shake. I looked him over as I shook his hand. He was just as square as us. He was standing there with his Polo shirt and blue khakis and matching loafers looking like he was straight out of a private school brochure. He was about six feet tall with low cut wavy hair. His skin was flawlessly smooth and chocolatey brown and his entire demeanor poured the words "I love the ladies." I didn't think he was a playboy. He actually seemed to care more about Shaniece than himself, but if that were the case, he wouldn't have had my cousin or my square ass in this house party in the P's surrounded by hard heads with hard legs and a burner on each hip.

"Pleased to meet you, David," I smiled. "Niecey, I'm just going to find myself a seat somewhere. Come and find me when you're ready to go." She nodded and got lost in David's eyes somewhere and I retreated to a corner across the room where I could keep an eye on her 'somewhere over the rainbow' in love ass.

I sat there in the corner halfway listening to this chick who was talking about her haters, although I had a strange suspicion that she actually didn't have any. Shaniece and David remained in the same spot as they talked and laughed and then became consumed by a kiss that seemed to be never-ending. The girl got up to go gossip with one of her friends about the other girls they came with just as some guy blew chunks into the kitchen sink because he couldn't handle whatever he had mixed together in his cup. I sat there in the corner alone, sufficiently entertained watching the circus of teenagers make a fool of themselves while trying to impress their friends.

"Excuse me," came a deep male voice entirely too close to my left ear for comfort. I jumped. "I'm sorry. My intentions aren't to bother you."

"I know, I know, but I'm just fine over here by myself," I told the guy, though I was definitely intrigued by him when our eyes connected. He was weirdly handsome to me, though his attention was quite unwelcome.

"I was just going to ask you…"

"To dance? Nah," I shook my head. "I don't dance, so save your breath. And I don't need a boyfriend either, so go ahead and enjoy the party. I'm fine in my little corner," I told him.

"It's cool if you don't dance. Honestly, I've been watching you since you came in," he admitted.

"Stalker much?" I frowned at him.

22

"Nah. I'm no stalker. There's just something about you. You have a beautiful smile, and I can see your intelligence in your eyes," he said. "You shouldn't have to sit here alone."

"It's okay. My cousin's here, so I thought I'd chill for a minute, but I don't usually do this. This isn't my type of party or my type of crowd. I won't be here long. You should just find one of the girls who's enjoying herself and showing off for attention."

"I'm not interested in the attention seekers, the gold diggers, or the thirst buckets. I've got my eyes on something much more special," he said as he licked his lips.

"Who? Me?" I laughed.

"Yes, you. You're beautiful," he said, the admiration evident in his voice. "You look like a black Barbie doll."

"Ha! Really?" I was amused.

"Seriously. You are perfect in every way. You want something to drink?"

"I don't really drink. Plus I don't even know what they have."

"C'mon," he stood and held his hand out for me to take. "Go in the kitchen with me."

"For what?"

"So you can see what they have to drink. It's a lot quieter

in there anyway. We won't have to shout over the music."

I stared at him for a few seconds, hesitant to take his hand, wondering if he was about to lead me to hell, trying to read any deceit or ill intentions hidden in his pupils. He seemed innocent and genuine, but I still had my doubts as I reached up and placed my hand in his. I looked him over from behind as he led me into the light of the kitchen. I glanced over my shoulder at my cousin who was still in the same spot, posted with David's lips on her neck and fingers up her skirt. She hadn't even noticed I had moved.

"What's your name?" he asked me as he leaned against the kitchen counter.

"Umm… Bre'ana," I said shyly, blushing slightly.

"Bre'ana, you're beautiful, sweetheart. You're absolutely gorgeous. I couldn't take my eyes off of you," he complimented me. "Your name has to mean something incredible."

"It means 'she ascends,'" I informed him.

"Really? That's amazing because you really do look like an angel."

"So, are you just going to stand here trying to run game on me, or are we actually going to have a real conversation? I could've stayed in my corner for this bullshit," I told him.

"Damn, shorty," he chuckled. "My bad."

"Make it your good next time," I rolled my eyes at him.

He actually was kind of handsome to me. He was tall with wide shoulders, and I could tell there were large muscles underneath his white t-shirt. He sipped from the red Solo cup in his left hand, and my eyes caught a glimpse of his gold teeth and the tattoos running down his left arm. He was a normal guy. He didn't have hazel brown or green eyes. His dreads weren't twisted from 'good hair.' He may not have even been cute to anyone else, but his swagger and thug appeal had me hooked. But as normal as he was, he was still abnormal.

"You're hard on a nigga," he told me. "I like that shit."

"I'm sure you're used to women just letting you have your way. I'm just not that chick. I'm generally uninterested." I said as I folded my arms across my chest.

"If you're so uninterested then why do you even try?"

"Try? I didn't try anything. You tried it," I corrected him.

"I'm saying though. You're so uninterested, but you put on a cute outfit, got your stomach all out, hair done, face beat, earrings and shit. What did you do all of that for if you're uninterested?" he questioned me.

"I knew we were coming to a party. I don't come out of the house looking just any kind of way. That's rule number one for a real lady."

"I feel you," he nodded. "But you looked at yourself in the mirror before you left the house, probably a half a dozen times."

"Of course I did, and I blew kisses at myself too," I snickered.

"Okay then. So you knew you were beautiful before you left the house, and you had to at least think someone else was going to think you were beautiful too."

"I can't be that beautiful. You're the only guy who thought I was. Nobody else has paid me any attention."

"Naw, shorty," he shook his head in disagreement. "I'm the only one who had balls enough to approach you. Believe me, I'm not the only one who noticed you sitting in that corner all by your lonely."

I was taken aback by the revelation and became suddenly self-conscious. He must've sensed it because he changed the subject.

"Do you want something to drink?" he asked as he waved his hand at the collection of half-empty bottles on the counter.

"I don't drink. I don't know what half of this shit is," I admitted.

"Well, there's vodka, tequila, rum, cognac, whiskey, bourbon..." he rattled off. I just looked at him like he was speaking a foreign language. I was still just as clueless as I was before he started talking. "Here, why don't you try some Bacardi," he suggested. "It's pretty light, and they've got a blender. If you pour it in the blender with some ice," he said as he dropped ingredients into the blender, "and some Jolly Ranchers, I heard it's pretty good." He turned the blender

26

on and once the contents were blended to his satisfaction, he poured them into a cup.

The moment I tasted it I loved it. The mixed fruit flavor of the candy mixed with the watermelon flavor of the alcohol was the perfect combination for my taste buds. Forgetting that I hadn't eaten anything in about seven hours, I downed the first cup within minutes and had my new friend, William Jefferson, Lil Will for short, pour the rest of the contents of the blender into my cup.

Our conversation seemed to take off from there. I had loosened up and become more comfortable with Lil Will, and he seemed to really like me. The music grew louder and I could feel the bass in my chest. I guess I blinked too long because when I opened my eyes again, I was on top of the kitchen counter twerking like a stripper with my shirt up around my neck. There were guys surrounding me, cheering me on and laughing continuously, but I had no desire to get down off the counter.

I bent over and touched my toes while shaking my ass and then dropped down on the counter into a split. The room erupted into a series of loud "ooohhh's" and I bounced my ass on the counter while still in the split. Somewhere deep down inside, the other me was shocked and appalled, unable to believe what the fuck I was doing. That bitch got pushed into a corner and told to have several seats while I let loose and my wild and free side was finally released, and she showed out with a vengeance.

Chapter 4

"So we're getting drunk at house parties and throwing that ass in a circle on kitchen counters now?" Shaniece's voice echoed in my head as I sat up in the bed. I looked around myself, unable to remember how I had gotten back to Shaniece's house. I felt like shit. My head was throbbing and my eyes could barely stay open.

"What are you talking about?" I asked her as I squinted in the direction of her voice, trying to look at her despite the pain in my eyes from the sunlight.

"Don't play with me, Bre. You know exactly what I'm talking about."

"I don't," I said as I shook my head. "I guess I must've been wasted, though, because I feel horrible."

"Wasted? Ha! Girl, you got white boy wasted at that party last night," she laughed.

"For real?" I was in disbelief. "What did I do Niecey?"

"I don't know what you were doing before I came into the kitchen, but I heard loud shouting and cheering and you weren't in that little corner you had been posted in, so I went in the kitchen and your ass was dancing like a stripper on the counter."

"What do you mean 'dancing like a stripper'?" I was hesitant to even ask.

"Well, when I came in the kitchen, you were bent over making your ass clap on the counter. Then you laid on your back and did that leg shaking thing that strippers do to make it clap, but when you tried to pussy pop on a handstand, I made you get your ass down and took you home," she explained.

"I did what?!"

"Yep, and judging by all the noise that was coming from the kitchen before I got in there, you were putting on quite a show."

"So how did I get home?" I frowned.

"David and that guy you were talking to, Lil Will, they helped me get you off the counter and to the car, and I drove us back home."

"Lil Will? I remember him. He was cute."

"Not really," Shaniece shook her head. "He was nice though."

"You didn't think he was cute?" I was almost offended.

"Not at all. Girl, the nigga got gold teeth and dreadlocks. Both of our moms would strangle our asses for being involved with someone like him."

"I know, but I like him. He's cute and he was really sweet

to me. I know he doesn't look like someone I should be with, but on the inside, he's a great guy," I explained.

"Well, he gave me his number to give to you…" she said in a sing-songy voice while holding the slip of paper between two fingers.

"Really?" I smiled widely, but Shaniece snatched the paper away as I reached for it. "Give it to me, Niecey. What's wrong with you?"

"Nope, nope," she shook her head as she held the paper in the air.

"Niecey, stop playing," I whined.

"I'll give you his number, but only if you promise to be careful. This isn't Memphis, Bre," she warned. "Men out here aren't always as they appear. He could be a great guy or he could be a wolf in sheep's clothing."

"Well, in his case, I think he's more of a sheep in wolf's clothing," I told her. "I promise, though," I said and she lowered the slip of paper into my palm.

"I'm serious, Bre'ana," she said in a low tone. "Please be careful. If you get caught up in this street life out here, you'll go home a completely different person. This shit will suck you in down here. I don't want anything to happen to you. I wouldn't be able to forgive myself."

"Even if something did happen to me, it wouldn't be your fault, but I promise to be careful," I told her. "Now let me lay down for a bit longer because my head is throbbing and I'm exhausted."

"All of that twerking…" she laughed.

"Whatever," I giggled and rolled back over.

*   ~   *   ~   *

When I finally texted Lil Will three days later, he was happy to hear from me. I immediately became addicted to his conversation. Shaniece and I would both post up in the lounge chairs by the pool and talk to David and Lil Will for hours at a time.

Lil Will was actually twenty-one. I couldn't figure out what he was doing at a high school party, but I was certainly glad that he was. He had his own apartment and his own car, and he made his own money. He loved the fact that I was in love with chemistry, biology, and math, and he often laughed how nerdy I was.

We talked and texted every day for two weeks before we saw each other again. Shaniece and I were on one of our weekend mall runs, talking and laughing, completely submerged in our own little world and oblivious to anything and anyone around us. We were walking through the food court sipping lemonade when a familiar voice came from behind us.

"Oh, but to be a straw between those lips, lightly bitten by the pearl of her teeth. To be the Styrofoam in her clutch, the cup in her grasp. I will not have known life until I find myself her play-toy or even her trash, used and tossed away. For she is the queen of the South, and Beauty is her name."

I spun around. Even if it had not been Lil Will, the sheer Shakespearean poetry of his words would've had me intrigued enough to pause my promenade through the mall. My eyes rested on his silhouette before they consumed his actual image. Red t-shirt, white jeans, red Gucci belt, red, white, and black Jordans. He must've had about a half a dozen chains around his neck, big shiny diamond nugget earrings that I could tell were real, three rings on each hand, and a watch on his left wrist that I'd bet half of my mother's salary was a real Rolex. He must have been the ringleader because he had a small entourage of about six guys with him who all looked confused and amused at what he had just said.

"How did you know it was me when you only saw me from behind? And how could you know if I was beautiful or not if you hadn't even seen my face yet?" I questioned him.

"First of all, I'd know that walk, that cute little giggle you do, and that firm ass anywhere. Second," he said as he approached me, "beauty is so much more than facial features. The beauty of a woman exists in the cloud of air around her. You can smell it in the scent of her flesh, and it lingers anywhere she has been. It leaves a trail that you can follow straight to her, and I followed your trail straight to you." He lifted my chin with his thumb and forefinger and kissed me gently on the lips.

Somewhere outside of the bubble that engulfed us, I heard Shaniece gasp and then a couple of the guys jeered and cheered. When he pulled away, I was speechless. All I could do was look at him and blush.

"You okay, Barbie doll?" he asked.

"Umm…yeah, yeah. I'm okay," I said quietly.

"It's nice to finally see you again," he smiled, exposing his gold teeth. "What have you two been up to?" he asked as he nodded in Shaniece's direction. One of his friends had walked over to Shaniece and attempted to run his game on her, but of course, she wasn't going.

"Nothing. Swimming and shopping, as usual," I said simply.

"How about you come and roll with me for a little while?"

"Uhhh…I don't know about that," I hesitated.

"Aw, c'mon. You're in good hands, and I'll have you home at a decent time," he said with pleading puppy dog eyes.

"Shaniece," I called my cousin over without breaking eye contact with Lil Will.

"What's up, Bre?" she asked as she stood next to me.

"Lil Will wants me to ride with him so he can show me the city," I told her.

"I don't know, Bre. You're pretty well acquainted with the city already," she folded her arms.

"If you want me to go with you," I told Lil Will, "you're

going to have to convince my twin cousin that I'll be in good hands."

"C'mon, baby. You know I'm not going to let anything happen to you."

"All I know is what you've been telling me on the phone, and it doesn't take shit to lie to someone you're not even face to face with," I said as I poked him in the chest.

"Well, I'm face to face with both of you now, and I'm looking you in your eyes and telling you that neither of you has anything to worry about," he said to me and then looked Shaniece in her eyes too.

"You'd better not let anything happen to her without it happening to you first," Shaniece warned him with squinted eyes.

"I guarantee you that I won't let any harm come her way," he told her.

"Bre, you call me if anything at all goes wrong. I don't care where you are. I'll come get you," she told me. I nodded and she hugged me and turned and walked off.

"Well, I guess I'm all yours now," I sighed nervously. "What's up?"

"C'mon," he said as he offered me his arm. "Let's get out of here."

It was early in the day. Lil Will drove me all over the

city and showed me all of the important landmarks, even Dr. King's childhood home, his church, and his final resting place. He showed me his neighborhood, and we even ate at a small restaurant he loved to frequent. People all over town were waving at him and speaking to him. I could tell he was popular, well-known, and well-liked, though it wasn't evident why. I enjoyed myself, and when we pulled into Aunt Sharon's driveway at eight-thirty that night, I wasn't ready to go inside, but I respected him more for bringing me home at a decent time.

"We should do this again. You should ride with me more often. You're great company," he told me. "Did you have fun?"

"Yes," I nodded. "I actually did enjoy myself."

"Good," he said as he smiled widely. "I'm glad. So can we do this again?"

I looked him in his eyes, searching for a need too urgent, a desire too desperate, but I only found a genuine curiosity that was perhaps too curious, but it was cute. There was something sincere in his eyes, something that I couldn't quite figure out, something that I felt like I had to figure out or I'd be missing something big.

"Yeah," I nodded shyly. "We can do this again."

"Great!" he said and then leaned over and kissed me long, deep, and gentle. At that moment I decided that I was his… completely.

Chapter 5

I started riding off with Lil Will two or three times a week. We'd just ride most days and talk about any and everything. Nothing was off limits. Politics, religion, the economy, fashion trends, music, school, the struggle.

Honestly, I knew nothing about 'the struggle.' I'd sit in the passenger seat of his Cadillac Escalade and just listen to him talk about the things he went through as a child while his mother struggled to feed and clothe him and his older brother Robert who had been killed two years before I met Lil Will by a stray bullet at a club. I couldn't imagine enduring the things that he had experienced as a child. I had never known what it's like to be hungry and not have food to eat. I had no clue what hand-me-downs were and had never worn clothes that were too small for me because we couldn't afford new clothes or clothes that were too big for me because an older sibling had outgrown them and I had to grow into them. I didn't know what gunshots sounded like outside of my bedroom window and I had never seen a real rat or roach in person.

The more he talked, the more it became evident that we were from two different worlds. It also became obvious, though, that Lil Will was desperately working to climb to the world I called my home. He didn't want to stay where he was. He wasn't comfortable there and had a hunger for a better life.

"Baby, there's a party tonight at one of my friend's houses. You wanna go with me?" he asked as we were riding around one night two weeks later.

"Sure. Can Shaniece come?"

"Umm, naw. How about you and I go? That way you can meet some of my friends. Shaniece can come next time," he told me.

"Well, can I go by the house and change clothes?"

"Naw, baby. Don't worry about it. You're straight with that on. You're good. You're with me," he assured me. I looked down at the simple white V-neck tee and blue jean shorts I had on, and Lil Will looked over at me. "Look, baby. If you really want to change, I'll take you to the mall to find something."

"But I-"

"No but's. It's all on me. You can have whatever you want in the whole mall," he told me.

"I've got my own money," I laughed. "I don't need you to buy my clothes for me."

"Oh, I know. I understand you've been raised to be independent and all, but I got you. I got this. Don't worry about it this time. We'll just put you an outfit together and I'll pay for it," he told me with his hand on my thigh.

* ~ * ~ *

Time slowed down as we entered the party. The party-goers seemed to dance in slow motion on the dance floor. The music and laughter all melted together to a low hum. I had never been to a party like this. The marijuana smoke was thick enough to have come from a fog machine. There were no frowns; no one was nervous, scared, or worried. Everyone was having a great time. I could feel Lil Will's eyes watching my reaction as we walked through the crowd. He slipped his fingers between mine and held my hand. It startled me and caught me off guard. We had never held hands in public, only in the car as we rode.

I told myself that this was our first public appearance as a couple. He was trying to make a statement. That's why I had on these high-waisted navy blue shorts with my ass cheeks hanging out of the bottom and this cream-colored top that dipped so low it almost dove into my shorts. That's why my hair was pinned up in a cute little style and my hoops were big enough to be bracelets. It was why I had on strappy six-inch heels and gold bangles up my arms. It was why he had convinced me to get a nose ring while we were shopping at the mall and why he had almost demanded that I wear his chain, insisting that it set off my outfit. He didn't just want me to look cute. He wanted me to look like I was his.

We walked straight through the crowd to the bar, still in slow motion, and I looked all around us. His plan had worked. I must've looked like I was his- or somebody's- because heads were turning, eyes were squinting in envy, mouths were left agape in wonder. I looked up into Lil Will's eyes and he smiled at me and nodded his head in approval.

"What do you want to drink?" he asked as we stood at the

bar.

"How about I just stick with what I know?" I suggested.

"Bacardi it is," he said and then ordered himself a Remy and Coke and me a Barcardi Ann Sheridan Cocktail. I had no idea what was in it, but when I tasted it I loved it. I had three of them before the DJ dropped "Rude Boy" and Lil Will dragged me onto the dance floor with my fourth cup sitting on the bar half empty.

"Baby, my drink," I protested.

"Fuck that drink. I'll buy you another. Dance with me. Put that ass on me, girl," he said as we stopped in the middle of the floor. I raised an eyebrow at him, taking it as a challenge.

Lil Will and I grinded for hours to every song the DJ played and lost track of time. We were in our own zone in a world where only he and I existed. The sunlight was blue there, and the moonlight was red. My eyes were closed, my hands were in the air, and I felt free from all worries, inhibitions, and expectations. We burst into laughter at the end of a song, and he wrapped his arms around me from behind. When I looked over my shoulder, our lips connected and I melted into him. I slowly turned to face him, kissing him back more deeply than before. His hand caressed my cheek as his other hand pulled me closer to him and I became putty in his hands.

He led me back to the bar as he pulled away from me. I was stopped in mid-stride by a sudden jerk on the top of my pants. Lil Will felt the resistance as well and we both turned around.

"Ugh! Stupid bitch!" a girl I had never seen before screamed as her fist connected with my lip. Caught completely off guard, my natural instinct kicked in and I began throwing punches back. "That's MY man, bitch!" she yelled as the crowd parted to give us room to fight, and her fist landed on my nose this time. I punched her in the eye and nose with a one-two punch, which startled her just long enough for Lil Will to jump in and attempt to break up the fight.

"Toya, what the fuck?!" he yelled as he tried to pull me back.

"Don't you 'what the fuck' me, Will! I come in here trying to enjoy myself with my girls to get my mind off of your dog ass, and here you are grinding with this bitch on the dance floor! You ain't never kissed me like that! And out in public?! For everybody to see?! And she got your chain on?!" she screamed.

"We ain't been together in months! I can do what the fuck I want!" he told her.

"Oh, you can? Well let's see how much you like your little ho after I beat her ass!" she screamed and then reached up and snatched me by my hair as three of her friends joined in punching, scratching, and kicking me.

"Ugh!" Lil Will's voice moaned in pain and he reached down and flung the girls in every direction to get them off of me.

"She ain't getting away that easy," the Toya girl said and lunged for me again, reaching for Lil Will's chain, but Lil

Will blocked her with a backhand to her face that sounded off. The crowd gasped, and Lil Will bent down and picked me up from the floor. I could only cover my face as he carried me in his arms out the door, leaving Toya and her flunkies strewn across the floor.

"Baby, I'm so sorry," he apologized to me as I sat crying in the car. I couldn't put together two words to say to him. "Baby, I'm sorry," he repeated when I didn't turn away from the window to face him and didn't respond.

"I've never been so humiliated in my life," I whimpered. "Fighting over a guy in a club like some common hoodrat. I should be ashamed."

"No, baby. It's not you, and it's not your fault," he said as he drove. "She attacked you. Of course, you were going to defend yourself."

"But she attacked me because of you," I turned to him and said. "Why didn't you tell me you had a crazy ex-girlfriend? Huh? Did you know she was going to be there?"

"No, I didn't know. Even if I did, that wouldn't have stopped me from going or bringing you. I just would've been more prepared."

"More prepared? More prepared for that kind of crazy?" I scoffed. "Nigga, there were four of them! They jumped me!"

"They had to jump you. That bitch can't fight, and she didn't know what she was up against. She wasn't going to win that fight against you, and her little buddies knew it, so they played the only card they had."

"Where are you going?" I asked as I looked around us. "Take me home."

"I'm not taking you home like this. Look at you."

"What do you mean you're not taking me home? Take me home, Will!"

"I'm not taking you home like this, Bre!" he yelled.

"Where are you taking me?"

"I'm taking you to my place to get cleaned up some, and then I'll take you home."

"Your place? Hell naw! You can just turn around and take me to the house. I'm not going home with you after you just got my ass whooped!"

"Bre, I'm sorry! I didn't get your ass whooped. That bitch's bitterness, loneliness, and jealousy are what got your ass whooped, Bre. There is no battle for you to fight because you've already won the war. Don't you see that? You won the moment we walked in there together holding hands. You won when I hugged you and kissed you in the middle of the dance floor. Didn't you hear her? I never took her anywhere with me in public. She's jealous, Bre. Don't you see how special you are to me? Can't you tell I don't treat you like anybody else I've ever been with? You ain't like those hos, Bre'ana. You're different in the best ways possible."

I just looked at him and then turned back to my thoughts out the window of the Escalade. I must have dozed off in the car because the next thing I remembered was sitting on the edge of an unfamiliar bed while Lil Will dabbed an alcohol-soaked cotton ball on a cut on my lip. I usually hated alcohol, but the burn felt good this time. He used a warm, wet cloth to wipe away the drops of blood on my face, and that's when I noticed he had a deep scratch that ran down the length of his left cheek. I picked up the cotton ball he had sat down and dabbed the scratch on his face. He winced in pain and then kissed me gently as we locked eyes.

I kissed him back, encouraging him. I had no idea what I was doing or even what I wanted to do. I just knew it felt good to have him so close to me, caressing me, kissing me. His tongue explored my mouth and then he gently pulled back on my bottom lip. I was caught up in the moment, lost in the passion.

Lil Will unbuttoned my shorts and slipped his hand down in my thong. I inhaled sharply at the sensation. I had never felt anything like that in my life. My eyes rolled back just with him rubbing on the outside, and when he slipped a finger inside, I finally understood what Shaniece had meant. It really was like an itch that I didn't even realize I had and couldn't scratch for myself.

"How does that feel, Baby Girl?" he whispered in my ear.

"It's… I… ohhh," I moaned. I couldn't gather my words. I could barely catch my breath.

"Does it feel good, baby?" he asked.

"I've never... ohhh... ahhh," I moaned.

"You never what?" he whispered to me.

"I've never done this. It feels so good," I told him. He stopped and stared at me. I frowned at him, not wanting him to stop.

"What do you mean? You've never been fingered before?" he asked me, worried about what my answer would be.

"I... I've never done any of this," I revealed. "I've never kissed anyone but you. Nobody has ever touched me down there, in there, anywhere around there."

"Baby... you're a virgin?"

"Umm... well, yeah," I shrugged my shoulders, slightly ashamed. I knew most girls my age had been having sex for a while and had plenty of stories to tell. I just wasn't like other girls.

"My God, baby! Why didn't you tell me? I would've been so much gentler. I didn't know, baby. I'm sorry."

"No, you didn't hurt me. It felt good," I assured him.

"But, baby, it's your first time... your first kiss. I should have made it so much more special than that. You should've told me, baby. I would've been so much more considerate than what I was," he insisted.

"Calm down, baby," I said as I caressed his cheek. "You

know now, so let's make it special now."

"Are you sure, baby? You don't have to do any of this if you're not ready," he said as he stared deep into my eyes, searching for the truth even if I didn't give it to him.

"I'm sure," I told him. He stared at me a few seconds longer, mostly in shock from what I could tell, and then took my face in both hands and kissed me again, this time with an urgency and a passion that he hadn't had before.

"If we're going to do this, I'm going to do it right," he said as he stood up and walked over to his nightstand. He pulled out a neatly folded piece of paper and unfolded it as he sat on the bed next to me. "I just got tested last month," he told me. "I'm completely clean. These are my test results," he said as he handed me the paper to read. I read the line of negative results and handed him the paper back. "I've... umm... never had sex with anyone without a condom," he admitted. "Is it okay if this is a first time for me too?"

I looked him in his eyes and felt like I couldn't deny him. I nodded and then said, "Make sure you pull out, though. No babies. Not yet." He nodded in agreement and kissed me again.

He laid me back on the bed, still kissing me. I was still inebriated from the Bacardi and my mind felt like it was swimming. Everything felt like someone had slowed down the tape again. Lil Will's lips inched down my neck and chest, placing kisses in a trail, marking his path. His fingers pulled my top up and over my head as he continued down, leaving kisses between my breasts and then down to my navel.

He slid my shorts off and then looked my body over in admiration like he was checking the progress of a detailed portrait he was painting. I could see the lust in his eyes. The desire was perched on his forehead, nestled deep between the strands of his eyebrows. I imagined him salivating, though I could tell he was trying to hide it. He was standing there trying to decide where to start. I must've looked like a snack to him because he looked like he wanted to eat me alive. I decided to help him out some. Unfastening my bra, I dropped it on the floor next to the bed, allowing my perky C-cups to fall free. Lil Will took that as an opportunity to wrap his lips around my left nipple as he rolled the right one between his thumb and forefinger until it was hard and extra sensitive.

There was something happening to me. I could feel the change in my body. I was feeling sensations I had never felt before that I could tell were creating feelings I had never even considered having. Lil Will looked up at me, observing the confused mixture of expressions on my face. He moved over me and kissed me again, and then pulled his own shirt over his head to reveal a chest and abdomen completely covered in tattoos. I heard his belt clink as it came unbuckled, but I was distracted by the tickling sensation of Lil Will's lips and tongue leaving large wet kisses down my sides.

His hands were all over me, and anywhere his hands were absent, his tongue was present. He ran his fingers over the thin material covering my virgin wetness and I sighed at his touch. He loved that shit. I could see it in his eyes. Slipping his fingers into the band, he pulled my pretty little lace thong down my thighs and slid it off my feet. He looked up at me, checking my reaction again, and then kissed my lips again to calm my uneasiness. He ran his fingers through my juices and then moved down between my legs.

From the moment his lips kissed me where my thighs met, I thought I was losing my mind. The tip of his tongue flicked across my clit, and I moaned "oh God" so weakly I sounded like a baby. Lil Will slid his arms underneath my thighs to hold them open and then dove in. I became short of breath as the sudden surge of pleasure rolled up my spine in waves and then subsided back down my hips. My fingers became tangled in his dreadlocks as I subconsciously pushed his face deeper into his plate. My mind was racing. All I could think about was that this was what I had been missing. This was why my friends had been sneaking out of the house in the middle of the night and why their boyfriends had been climbing through their bedroom windows. This was what all of the fuss was about. I finally understood.

When he finally came up for air, my back was curled into a permanent arch and I was breathing so hard I was sure I had become asthmatic. He stood up and dropped his jeans. I could see the bulge in his boxers and I was nervous about what was hidden behind the plaid-printed cotton. He watched me watching him as he stepped out of his bedazzled True Religions and tossed them aside. He stared straight into my eyes as his boxers slid to the floor. There it was. I had absolutely nothing to compare it to, but I was confused. Whoever had come up with the name Lil Will for him obviously had never seen what I was seeing. He didn't have a weenie, a ding-a-ling, or "junk" like my schoolmates called it. This mad had a penis, a full dick, and there was nothing little about it. I was intimidated, and I knew he could see it written all over my face.

Our lips were reunited as he laid on top of me. He had quickly learned that was the one sure way to calm and comfort me. His fingers caressed my cheek as his dreadlocks fell loosely around our faces like curtains, closing us into our own little world. He looked into my eyes as he lined the head of his dick up with my waiting warmth. He paused for a moment, allowing me one last chance to change my mind, but my mind was made up. He had taken me to a place I had never dreamed of going and walked me to the door. Now I was ready to go inside.

He slipped it inside and I cringed. Inch by inch until he was halfway inside, I could tell he was trying not to hurt me, but once he got that far in I felt a sudden jolt of pain that caused me to tense up. He was hitting something that was blocking him. I was lost, but I could tell he wasn't.

"Baby," he whispered, "bear with me for a minute because this is going to hurt. I'm about to pop your cherry."

I nodded in understanding and he wove his fingers between mine. I held my breath as I felt him pull back and then shove it back in. I gasped and fought back a scream. Will pumped into me over and over and my nails dug into his flesh as I writhed in pain. He didn't just pop my cherry. He demolished the damn thing. Once he was satisfied that nothing was in his way, he slowed down again and stroked me more gently. My buzz was gone; the pain had killed the alcohol. I had tears in my eyes and my nails had made imprints in his hands.

Whoever said pleasure comes after the pain really knew what they were talking about. I began feeling sweet sensations mixed with the stinging pain. I felt crazy like I was having a psychotic break. I could feel my face wincing and then sighing. My body couldn't decide which sensation was stronger and was doing an incredible impression of Dr. Jekyll and Mr. Hyde. Will's stroke slowed even more, and the pain began to subside until I was only feeling pleasure.

I felt like a completely different person. I understood every music video, every sex scene in the movies, every wedding, every argument. Visions flashed in my mind of me slow dancing for him, me bouncing on Will's dick like I knew what I was doing, Will pulling my hair as I was bent over a bathroom sink.

"Oh God, Will!" I moaned out loud, and he kissed me as he lifted one of my legs and wrapped it around his waist.

My breathing grew heavy again as he hit something deep inside of me that felt like he was pressing a button marked "Yes" over and over. I had watched enough movies to know that this must have been what a moan was all about. This was the source of the tears in the corner of a woman's eyes and the reason for a man's eyes rolling into the back of his head. I had discovered why men kill for women and why women break into senseless catfights over men. I understood the sexiness of a man's sweaty back and the beauty of a woman's distorted face.

My body fell into a rhythm with Will's stroke as I moved with him and encouraged him. His lips grazed my neck, fell against my jawline, and then tumbled down to my shoulder blade. I could feel his eyes watching me and my reactions, his gaze burning the side of my face, his eyes calling out for me to look into them. It almost felt forbidden or deadly, as though if I looked into his eyes they would turn me into stone like Medusa's. So I avoided them by closing my eyes.

His stroke continued as he wrapped his lips around my nipple while he held my entire breast firmly in the palm of his hand, causing fireworks to shoot down my spine. My other leg wrapped itself around Will's waist and my ankles locked together. He stroked for a few more minutes and then eased up and asked me to turn over and lay on my stomach.

"Baby, I'm bleeding," I told him as I looked down while turning over.

"I know, baby. I popped your cherry. It's your first time. You're supposed to bleed."

"But it's getting all over your sheets."

"Baby, I've got other sheets," he chuckled. "It's okay."

I laid on my stomach with my head on his pillow and closed my eyes. He kissed up my back, landing on the nape of my neck as he slid his dick back inside of me and I cried out.

"Am I hurting you, baby?" he asked in a panic.

"No, baby," I whined. "It feels so good."

I felt the wind of his breath as he exhaled in relief. I purred like a kitten as he slid in and out of my wetness. I could feel him against my walls and as he dipped deep into the bottom. Releasing soft grunts in my ear, Will sped up his rhythm and my moans grew louder.

"Will!" I moaned as my body shook slightly and the sensations I was feeling began to change.

"Does it feel good, baby?" he asked. I could tell by his voice that he had zoned out.

"Yes, baby, but I think I gotta pee."

"You don't have to pee, baby. You're about to nut."

"But…but…I don't know what that is. I don't know what that means," I whined nervously.

"Just relax, baby. Let go and allow the feeling to take over you. It's the best feeling in the world. It's the whole purpose of doing this, the goal we're working towards," he explained. "Just relax, baby," he whispered as he kissed my cheek.

"Willllll…" I moaned. "I'm scared. I've never felt anything like this."

"It's okay, baby. You trust me, don't you?"

"Yes," I whispered.

"Well, let go then. Fall into the feeling. It's the best feeling ever, baby. Calm down before the feeling goes away because it's hard to get it to come back once it leaves," he told me.

I couldn't calm down. The sensation itself was causing my heart to beat rapidly. The fear of the feeling combined with the worry and nervousness of it being my first time to create an overwhelming excitement that I couldn't even begin to describe. Will's lips felt good against my face; his fingers felt good against my arms. I closed my eyes again and melted into the boiling lava that was rising from my core.

Will could tell I was trying and that my tension was beginning to wear off. His speed picked up again and he struck something deep inside of me that made me moan even louder as my eyes popped open in shock.

"Baby!" I called out. "Ah! Baby! Will!"

"That's it, baby. I feel it. Let it come," he whispered.

"Ugh! Will! Will! Willlllll!" I screamed as my eyes rolled back and I was looking at my own thoughts. I watched roses blossom as if their speed was on fast-forward. The sun rose over a mountaintop, and confetti fell in Times Square. My entire body was overcome with the blazing heat of a hundred hells hushed by the wind of a thousand moons. My back arched and my muscles contracted, and I both felt and heard a sudden gush of fluids release from the very center of me. Will released a deep grunt, snatched his dick from my womb, and shot juices all over my ass cheeks. He collapsed next to me, both of us huffing and puffing with heavy breathing.

"Oh God, baby," I whimpered.

"I know. I know," he said as he pulled my hair back and kissed me and then got up and went into the bathroom. He came back with a warm wet towel and wiped all of his juices off of my ass. I turned over onto my back to face him, and he cleaned my inner thighs of the traces of blood smeared across them. "C'mon," he said with an outstretched hand. "I know you're tired," he said as he looked at my reluctant face, "but come and get in the shower with me."

I rose from the bed and took his hand, allowing him to lead me into the bathroom. He turned on the shower and allowed the water to warm up while he grabbed towels and shower gel from the closet as well and pinned my hair up for me and then helped me into the shower, stepping inside behind me.

Will faced me in the shower. He stood there just looking at me in awe and I wished I could read his mind and know what he thought of me at that moment. Suddenly, he took my face in his hands and kissed me forcefully, deeply, sincerely. My hand reached up to caress his cheek as well, and he winced in pain again. I touched the scratch on his cheek, sadness in my eyes. Will turned me around to face a mirror hanging on the shower wall. Wiping the mirror with a towel that had been hanging on the shower door, he bent down so that we were cheek to cheek. I had a matching scratch on my left cheek too. I turned and looked him in his eyes and then kissed him again.

Chapter 6

"I can't believe you were gone all night like that! You'd better be glad my mom had to work today or you would've been in big trouble if she came up here to wake you for breakfast and you weren't here," Shaniece fussed at me as we sat in front of the TV eating cereal the next afternoon. "You should've at least called me so I could cover for you," she continued.

"I know, Niecey. My bad," I said nonchalantly.

"So are you going to tell me what happened or not?"

"Not! It's none of your business," I told her.

"None of my business?" she said offended. "Bre, we tell each other everything. Since when is anything none of my business?"

"Since you started keeping stuff from me," I told her.

"But, Bre, I told you everything. Just because I didn't tell you as soon as it happened doesn't mean I kept it from you. I just saved it all until you came down here."

"Niecey, if you weren't going to tell me about David fingering you, you would've never told me about your kissing escapades," I said as I turned and frowned at her.

"But, shit, Bre! I thought you had already probably passed that stage. I didn't want to call you with something I thought you'd think was so trivial," she admitted.

"Why would you think I was past that stage?" I frowned. "I call you and tell you everything. You know shit Chloe doesn't even know. Why wouldn't I call and tell you about my first kiss?"

"I mean, you're older than me…."

"I'm only two days older than you, Niecey! That shit doesn't even count! We're the same age!" I stopped her. "You can't use that as an assumption that I'm doing anything that I haven't told you I'm doing. There are girls years younger than us at my school that are doing shit our parents aren't even doing. Age doesn't mean shit, Niecey."

"I guess I just assumed you had kissed a guy before and just hadn't gotten around to telling me or maybe it had slipped your mind," she said with a shamed look on her face.

"No, Niecey," I said as I shook my head. "I tell you everything within twenty-four hours of it happening. Even if I only get a chance to text you what happened, I always tell you and then give you the details later. I don't withhold anything from you."

"Except this, huh?" she said with her sadness dripping from her voice. "What is this? Some kind of punishment or repayment for not telling you about the kisses?"

"You keep asking me what happened as if something actually happened."

"You keep hiding it as if there's actually something to hide," she shot back.

"What makes you think there's anything to tell?"

"Bre, you stayed out all night. You came in here at noon and got straight in the shower, so I'm wondering what you're washing off. You're not in the bed in hibernation, so I'm wondering where you slept. Shit, you're wide awake. You've got on make-up fresh out of the shower, so I'm wondering what you're trying to cover up." Her eyes narrowed at me. Shaniece knew me better than my own best friend. I knew I couldn't hide anything from her.

"If I tell you what happened you have to promise not to flip out on me," I sighed in defeat.

"When have I ever flipped out on you?" she asked with pursed lips. "I knew something happened. C'mon! Spill the beans!"

"Will and I were out riding around like we always do, and he asked me to go to a party with him."

"What was it? A slumber party?" Shaniece interrupted.

"Shaniece, are you going to let me tell the story?"

"My bad. Guess I'm doing the same thing you were doing when I was telling you about David," she chuckled.

"Pretty much," I smirked. "So he took me to the mall and I got all dolled up, got my makeup done at the Mac counter, even got my nose pierced with a real diamond stud," I told her.

"I noticed. It's cute. Fits your face," she complimented me.

"Thanks. So he got sexy as hell too though. He was all dressed up, looking like a snack and shit," I giggled. "And he had me wear his chain. So we went to the party. I could tell it was a different atmosphere when I walked in. It was a drama-free, everybody having fun type of party. I had like four or five drinks and then Will pulled me onto the dancefloor. So we danced and danced for hours, and then he kissed me- like really kissed me- in front of everybody at the end of one of the slow songs. We headed back to the bar, but this girl attacked me..." I recounted.

"Attacked you? A bitch put her hands on you, Bre?" Shaniece was livid.

"Yeah, her and her friends. They jumped me and Will slung them off of me and back-handed the girl who was his ex and then picked me up and carried me to his truck."

"Girl, he should've beat her ass," she mumbled.

"Nah, the slap hurt her feelings enough. That shit sounded off loud as hell. I knew she was embarrassed."

"So what happened after that?" Shaniece asked as she shoveled Fruity Pebbles into her mouth.

"He took me back to his place because he didn't want to bring me here with my face all messed up."

"And?"

"Well," I huffed at her persistence, "he cleaned up the little bit of blood I had on my face, kissed me, and then he fingered me," I told her. She gasped.

"For reeeeeeaaalll? How was it?"

"Amazing," I confessed. "It was the most amazing thing I've ever felt until…" I hesitated about telling her everything.

"Until what?" Shaniece egged me on, but I couldn't even make eye contact with her. "Until what, Bre?" I just stared into my bowl of Cocoa Puffs. "Bre?!" she yelled as she slapped my arm. When I didn't look up at her, she gasped again. "Bre, y'all didn't! You're lying!"

"How can I be lying and I haven't said anything?"

"That's the point. Your silence was an insinuation."

"Well, the silence would pass the lie detector test."

"Oh, my God! Bre!" she squealed as she covered her mouth with both hands. I couldn't tell if she was proud or entertained, but she certainly wasn't mad or disappointed like I knew our parents would be if they found out.

"Yeah, we did," I said and nodded.

"You've got to tell me everything!" She plopped down on the floor next to me.

"What do you want to know? He fingered me and then he took my clothes off. He ate it and then made love to me."

"You make that shit sound so simple. Weren't you scared?"

"I was still drunk, so I was more nervous than scared," I admitted.

"Did it hurt?"

"Hell yeah! It hurt like hell, especially when he popped my cherry, but he told me when he was about to pop it so I'd know it was going to hurt."

"Damn, Bre. He sounds like a real gentleman."

"He was. He was extra gentle and very considerate. He didn't even care that I bled all over his sheets. When we got out of the shower, he changed the sheets and we laid down. He wrapped his arms around me and we fell asleep."

"Wow, Bre. So are y'all together now?"

"Honestly, we were together the moment he put his chain around my neck. We walked into that party holding hands and he kissed me in front of everybody. It was his way of showing everyone that we're together. It's also what he ex was mad about because she was ranting that he never did any of that with her," I explained.

"Damn, Bre. Just...I know it's a little late for this, but make sure y'all be careful. I told you about guys down here, and you have to remember that you're only here for the summer. What are y'all going to do when you have to go back home? And did y'all use protection? Y'all used a condom, right?"

"Don't be bombarding me with questions, Niecey," I laughed. "We haven't talked about what we'll do during the school year, but I'm sure we'll figure something out. And no, we didn't use a condom. I made him pull out."

"Oh my God, Bre! Have you lost your mind? Did he actually pull out?"

"Yes, he did. What's the problem?"

"You could've gotten pregnant. You should've used a condom. He could've had an STD or anything could've gone wrong," she ranted.

"Relax, Niecey. He showed me his test results. He's clean. Stop with the what-ifs. Everything is perfectly fine, and I'm not pregnant," I told her.

"You just make sure you be careful, Bre. I warned you about these guys down here. Don't get caught up," she warned as she got up and went to the kitchen to put her bowl in the sink.

"I've got everything under control," I assured her.

"Yeah, well, you bring your ass upstairs so I can see what

you look like underneath the Mac," she said over her shoulder as she started up the stairs.

"Alright. Here I come."

* ~ * ~ *

Will and I were together all the time after that night. We were like Suge and Ms. Celie; Will was like honey, and I was like a bee. I wanted to follow him everywhere. I only had a few weeks left before I had to return home, and I tried to make the most of it by spending as much time as I could with Will. On nights when I spent the night at his place, I'd be sure to bring a change of clothes with me. Shaniece would cover for me with Aunt Sharon who didn't ask many questions anyway.

We were like rabbits; we both just wanted to have sex all the time. We couldn't get enough of each other. It took a few times for my nervousness and fear to wear off, but once they finally did, I was completely comfortable with Will.

He would call me his Barbie doll. He said I was so perfectly beautiful and he could always bend me any way he wished because of how flexible I was. So I started wearing pink all the time, just like Barbie, and I'd let him undress me like he was my Ken.

One night we were lying in his bed after the third time making love that day, and he said we needed to talk. So we both sat up in the bed and I sat between his legs with my head resting on his chest as he stroked my hair.

"I know we're in our own little bubble right now, and I don't want to interrupt our vibe," he said, "but it's almost time for you to go back home."

"We've got a whole week left before I leave," I told him.

"I know, but I feel like we should decide what we're going to do while you're gone back to Memphis for the school year. I've been thinking a little bit about it, and I wanted to bring it up early in case we didn't see eye-to-eye on things and got into an argument because I don't want you to leave mad at me so I wanted to have time to make it right," he explained.

"Why would I be mad at you?" I asked as I frowned at him over my shoulder.

"Bre'ana," he started, which immediately caught my attention. He never used my full name. "I want you to under-stand that you're going to be a few hundred miles away from me. We're both still young. I don't want to hold you back from anything back home."

"Wait...are you...are you breaking up with me?"

"Bre, I-"

"Will, you're not holding me back from anything. I'm going to go to school and do everything I'm supposed to do at home, and I'll be back next summer. We can text and talk on the phone every night," I told him.

"But, Bre, there are going to be boys at school that you're going to be interested in-"

"Oh, please! Don't you think if I was interested in them I would have been with them already?" I frowned. "I only have eyes for you." I kissed him gently.

"But, Bre, what about me? You may think you're not going to get those urges, but, baby, look how much we've been having sex. You're going to want to do it. And I'm realistic. I know I'm going to want to fuck, but I don't want to disrespect you either."

I just looked at him in disbelief of what I was hearing. I was disgusted and offended, and I knew he could read it all over my face.

"So this whole thing is about you being able to fuck whoever you want to while I'm gone back to school? For real, Will? Are you serious?"

"Baby, you've got to understand. I'm a grown ass man. I have needs," he tried to explain.

"Well, bring your ass to Memphis to see me then. I know the distance is going to be hard, Will, but there are ways to deal with all of that."

"So you're saying it's okay for me to come up to Memphis to see you?"

"Of course! I play rugby and volleyball. You can come to the games. You can come on the weekends and I'll link up with you," I told him. "Where there's a will there's a way."

"I can't come every weekend, but I'll come as often as

I can. I can't promise you anything, Barbie doll, but I'll do what I can, and we'll see how it works."

"I'll start coming down here more often too so that it won't all be on you. We'll make it work, baby. Watch. Everything will be just fine."

Chapter 7

Will and I made it through my junior and senior years in high school doing exactly as we planned. We talked on the phone almost daily and texted all the time. In addition to my yearly summer vacation in Atlanta, I also visited during Thanksgiving and Spring Breaks. Will came to Memphis for the first time about a month into my junior year. He got a nice hotel room downtown, and I spent the entire weekend with him. He started driving to Memphis one weekend every month except the months when I visited him. He even made a few of my championship games.

Over the course of those two years, I watched Will's dreadlocks inch down his back. He must have changed a dozen cars, and I never saw him in the same outfit or pair of shoes twice. He had his permanent gold teeth removed and replaced with a twenty-four karat gold, platinum, and diamond grill. He brought all kinds of gifts with him when he came to visit, and he always made sure he took me to an expensive restaurant on the Saturday night he was in town.

I felt special. I felt loved. When I was alone with Will, he made me feel like I was the most beautiful girl in the world. I felt so lucky to have found the perfect guy for me so early in life. It was a relief. I didn't have to deal with the stress of dating and dumping that all of my friends were enduring.

I went to prom with a group of my friends. Afterward,

Will picked me up, and I spent the night at his hotel room. My parents knew nothing about Will, but they never pressured me about dating or questioned me about staying out. When Will was in town, I'd tell them I was spending the weekend at Chloe's and there were never any further questions. Everything was perfect.

My father insisted that I take both the ACT and the SAT. My scores came back, and when he saw I had scored a thirty-four on the ACT and a twenty-two ninety-seven on the SAT, he assumed I would want to go to one of the Ivy League schools. Instead, I insisted on going to Georgia Tech to complete my undergraduate studies in their chemical engineering program. My father was furious. As prestigious as Georgia Tech was, it still was not good enough for his precious baby girl. I assured him that it was just for undergrad, just for my first degree. I'd get other degrees…Master's…Doctorate's… and he has his proud moment being the father of an Ivy League Valedictorian.

My mother told him to let me go, citing Atlanta's rich African-American history and culture which she said would make me well-rounded and help me to develop a real sense of self. Because of my test scores and academic history, I was offered a full scholarship. My mother argued that because it was not costing them any money, I should be allowed to choose where I desired to obtain my education. Of course, my father was still unmoved and highly dissatisfied, and he still required a considerable amount of reassurance and coercion because he would have gladly paid cash for my education if it meant I would receive a quality education from a reputed institute of academia. He had in fact been setting aside money for me to go to college and had enough to cover at least twelve years. My mother broke down the situation to him to the point where she finally had to tell him quite bluntly that I was of a legal age to make my own decisions and essentially there was nothing they could do to prevent me from going. Their wisest choice would be to support me in all of my endeavors and wish me the best so that I may begin my journey into independence and adulthood feeling loved and supported rather than worrying about my parents' disappointment and discontent.

So instead of paying for my education, my father paid up the rent on a beautiful two bedroom apartment for a year and furnished it with high-quality furniture.

"Bre'ana, if you choose to stay down here," he told me the day I moved in, "I'll come down here every year and extend your lease and pay your rent for the next year. If you decide you need to move, just let me know, and we'll relocate you to a place you find more suitable. And remember," he whispered while my mother was putting the last of the dishes in the kitchen cabinets, "Harvard is waiting for you; you're not waiting for Harvard. If you ever need me, sweetie, I'm just one call away." With that, he kissed my forehead, hugged me tightly, and told my mother he'd be waiting in the car.

My mother finished putting away the dishes as I sat at the kitchen island sipping orange juice. She gave me a quick speech about men, condoms, and having children out of wedlock, kissed my cheek, hugged me even tighter than my father had, and as she left out of the door, she told me how much she loved me and how proud of me she was.

My parents hadn't been on the road headed home for an

hour when my doorbell was rung by my first visitor. I opened the door. He was still tall, still had wide shoulders, and still had large muscles underneath his white t-shirt. The tattoos on his left arm were greased and his dreads were freshly twisted and braided. His eyes were hidden behind a pair of Ray-ban sunglasses, but his bejeweled teeth glistened at me when he smiled. He stepped inside and wrapped his arms around my waist, kicking the door closed as he walked me backward.

"Welcome to Atlanta, baby," he whispered in my ear as he laid me down on the bed, lifted my skirt, and slipped his tongue inside of my thong

* ~ * ~ *

I began my life in Atlanta with my head in the books during the day and my skirt up over my navel at night. Some days it seemed like I couldn't get out of class fast enough for Will. He'd already be texting me while I was crossing the parking lot going to my car. There were days that I'd come home after class and he'd be waiting for me in the parking garage or there would be a bouquet of roses in front of my door. We'd go to an occasional party and we'd spend long Saturday nights cuddled on the couch watching movies.

We were dozing off while watching old movies one night when there was a knock at Will's door. He glanced at the time on the screen of his phone, frowned, and then got up when the knocking turned into banging. He scoffed as he looked through the peephole and then turned around to return to the couch. Five steps into his retreat, the door busted open and in stormed Toya.

"So this is why you haven't been answering my calls?" she yelled when she saw me.

"Toya, what the fuck are you doing here?" he growled.

"What do you mean what the fuck am I doing here? I was damn near living here a couple of months ago. Oh, am I no longer welcome here?" she asked in an overly-dramatic tone. "Is this what happens when your little whore comes into town?"

I was speechless. I had never felt so disrespected and degraded in my life. Their arguing continues as an echo in the background of my thoughts. I heard nothing else that was said between them. I simply stood up, grabbed my jacket, and headed for the door. It wasn't until I passed the two of them that I was snatched back to reality by Will's hand on my arm and his voice calling my name, asking me to stay.

"Bre, huh? Like the cheese? Oh, this bougie bitch thinks she's Italian now, huh?" the dumb bitch laughed.

"First of all, you ugly," I said calmly. Will burst into laughter. "Second of all, the cheese is French, not Italian. Third, just because I'm not a fucking stalker and I'm not loud, obnoxious and ghetto does not mean I'm bougie. It means I have class. Class, you know? Like, umm, what they have at schools," I scoffed mockingly.

"Oh, you did not just call me ghetto!" Never mind me calling her ugly, right?

"Bitch, yes! Ghetto! What would be a better word for a

gum-smacking, weave patting, neck rolling bitch like you?" I looked at Will over my shoulder and said, "I'm out of here."

"No, baby. Please don't-"

"'No baby'? 'Please don't'?" Toya repeated. "So you begging this bitch now? Will, baby, you ain't never had to beg me for shit," she said as if that made her more enticing.

"Hmph! Obviously!" I said as I snatched away from Will's grip and headed for the door.

"Ho, you ain't gone keep insulting me!" Toya said as she approached me from behind.

"Before you run up on me, you'd better remember," I said as I faced her and stepped within an inch of her nose. "I have a mean left hook and none of your little entourage is here to help you," I said quietly, but sternly. Her facial expression showed that she remembered that I was good with my hands. "'Insulting', huh? That's more than five letters. Impressive," I said with a chuckle, and then turned to walk away.

"Bre..." Will called out. I could see the pleading in his eyes when I turned around.

"She damn near lives here, right? I have my own house. I don't need another woman's home."

I could hear their arguing in the parking lot as I got into my car. Some of Will's neighbors were standing outside peeking out of their doors, amused by the ruckus coming from his apartment. By the time Will came out of his apartment to look for me, I was pulling out of the parking lot into the Atlanta night.

*   ~   *   ~   *

"Bre! Bre!" Will was knocking at my door three days later after I had been ignoring all of his calls and texts. He had inboxed me on Facebook and dm'd me on Instagram, and I had refused to open any of his messages. "Bre! Bre, I know you're in there. I saw your car in the garage."

"Go away, Will!" I shouted from inside of the apartment.

"Bre, baby, open the door! Let me in. Let's talk about this," he sounded like an old begging Keith Sweat song.

"Ain't shit for you to say to me, Will. Go on back over there to your little live-in wifey and leave me the fuck alone," I yelled from the other side of the door.

"Baby, I don't want her! Please just hear me out, Bre."

"I don't want to hear shit you have to say. Now stop all that damn yelling and go away!"

"Bre, please! Don't do me like this!" I could hear the tears in his voice. "I love you!"

Time stood still. Everything around me just stopped. The birds were floating in mid-air. The second hand on my wall clock froze. The movie that was playing on the TV paused. I gasped.

I couldn't believe what I had just heard. What did he just say? I had to have heard him wrong. Was he bullshitting me? I bet myself that he couldn't say that to my face.

"What did you say?" I asked him with the door cracked.

"I said I love you, Bre'ana," he said more calmly. A look of relief washed over his face as I opened the door. He walked in and I closed and locked the door.

"You don't love me, Will. You can miss me with all of that 'I love you' bullshit. I may not be experienced at this love and relationship shit, but I know this shit you've been doing is not love," I told him.

"I do love you, Bre," he insisted. "I just missed you so much," he whined and tried to run his hand up my thigh, but I slapped it away.

"Yeah, you missed me so much that you started back fucking the same crazy bitch that jumped on me at a party. You missed me so much that you starting fucking the bitch on a routine basis, so much so that the bitch was nearly living with you. That's how much you missed me, though. Right?" I blasted him. "You missed me so much that you came to visit me every month and deserted your blessed side chick for the weekend. You even got rid of all signs of her presence when I came down here to visit you. If that's what happens when you miss me, then miss me less, nigga."

"Bre, baby, you've got it all wrong!"

"No, no. I'm pretty sure I have it right. You've fallen in

love with me. Right? You love me soooooo much. Well if this is the kind of love you dish out, baby, I don't need it in my life," I told him with my arms folded across my chest.

"But I need you, baby. I need you in my life, by my side. You give me a reason to go on, a reason to live. Don't you see that?"

"I give you a reason to live? Are you serious, Will? Do you hear yourself?" I asked as I plopped down on the couch ready to burst into laughter.

"Don't you dismiss me, Bre'ana!" he said. I had offended him. Good. Mission accomplished. Now it was time to make him suffer.

"Why did you come over here, Will? Do you know how much of an idiot you sound right now? You took my virginity when I was sixteen. We made an agreement that we'd try to make things work in a committed long-distance relationship. I would come to visit you and you would come to visit me. Somewhere along the way, you felt it would be okay for you to have a bitch at home that you're fucking on a regular basis and come and fuck me once a month or so. So now, I've moved down here to be close to you while I go to school, and the whole bunch of bullshit has blown up in your face. You've been spending all of this time with me, don't put the bitch out of your house, and now she done blew up your spot. And you really think I'm supposed to be understanding of this shit? You think I'm supposed to forgive you and take you back and act like nothing happened. This is the same bitch that jumped on me because I was dancing with you at a damn party. And to top all of that off, you have your ass standing at my damn door yelling and shit, putting my neighbors all in my business!" I felt like Jody on Baby Boy. I knew how nosey my neighbors could be and I knew they were all peeking their heads out of their doors to see what Will was yelling about.

"But, Bre-"

"Get the fuck out of my house, Will!" I screamed.

"Bre, listen-"

"Get the fuck out!"

"No! I'm not going until you listen to me," he declared as he grabbed my shoulders. "Bre'ana, I do love you. It's not that I don't love you, baby. We were apart for long periods of time, and I'm a grown man, baby. I had needs and urges that had to be satisfied and sometimes it just couldn't wait until you came down here on break. I honestly didn't want to fuck with her, Bre, but at least I know her. At least it wasn't a bunch of random hos I met in clubs. I was just using her for sex. That's it. I just needed someone to take up your slack until you got down here. Don't you see you're all I need, baby?" he said as he looked me in my eyes. "We haven't had any kind of problems since you've been here. I love you," he said and then kissed my neck and shoulder. "I love me some you. I don't need anybody else as long as I have you by my side."

Kween Pen

Organized Crime: Bacardi Barbie

KWEEN PEN

Kween Pen

Organized Crime: Bacardi Barbie

KWEEN PEN

Organized Crime: Bacardi Barbie

Kween Pen

Organized Crime: Bacardi Barbie

Chapter 8

I don't know why I believed him, but I did. Call me young, dumb, and naïve, but I was head over heels in love with Will and I believed that he would be faithful to me and I was all he needed. Though my eyes were blind to his infidelities, they were no longer blind to any other aspect of his life.

Will had never told me what he did for a living. He had his own place, a bunch of cars, nice clothes, and was always rolling in cash, but I had never questioned him or even bothered to ask what he did for a living. But one day, it came and found me at his front door. Literally.

Will had asked me to come over to his house for dinner and a movie that Saturday night to celebrate my great scores on my final exams and the end of my freshman year. He had promised to cook his lasagna that I loved so much and make a salad and garlic bread to go with it. I had an unopened bottle of Bacardi at my apartment that Will had brought over a few weeks before. We had fallen asleep before we got a chance to open it that night, so I brought it along with me to make mixed drinks to go with dinner.

I had parked in my usual parking spot, but as I walked down the sidewalk to his building, I could hear male voices involved in an argument.

"C'mon, man. You know I'm good for it," the first voice

said.

"Good for it? You're already two hundred dollars in debt with me. The only thing you're good for is a bullet or a beat down," the second voice, which sounded like Will's voice, said.

"C'mon, Will, man. I gotchu man. I gotchu. Soon as I get my check," the first voice pleaded.

"Mother fucker, you get your check and don't nobody see you or hear from you for a whole week. By the time you turn back up, you're coming down off a high and broke as fuck. You ain't gone get shit else out of me until you pay up, nigga, and that better be soon or I'm going to come and find your mother fucking ass," I heard Will threaten the first guy.

"Will, man, I gotchu. I gotchu!"

"You already said that shit, nigga. I'm tired of hearing that bullshit. I don't play about my paper. Now you go find my money and don't bring your ass back to my mother fucking house. You know when and where to find me."

I turned the corner to see Will standing just outside of the door of his apartment watching a middle-aged white guy walk off. The man looked directly at me with red eyes as he passed me. His tan and green plaid button down was just as filthy as the blue jeans and old New Balance tennis shoes he was wearing. His hair was long and unkempt, and his face was covered in hair that was spotted by open sores. Will looked at me and tried to play it off with a smile.

"Hey, baby. C'mon in. Dinner's just about done," he greeted me with a peck on my cheek.

"Will," I said as I sat the bottle on the kitchen counter and he closed and locked the door.

"Yeah, baby?"

"Come here," I said as I sat down on the sofa.

"Oookaaayyy," he said, and then sat next to me. "What's up, Barbie doll?"

"We've been together for quite a long time now, and I've never asked you what it is that you do for a living. Like…I honestly have never asked you how you make your money. What's even funnier to me is that you never volunteered that information either. Most people have some kinds of stories about something that happened at work when they come home every day. Most people have co-workers that they're best friends with and co-workers that they're itching to catch off of the premises. They have check stubs and W-2's, and they file taxes. But, Will, I've never seen you in a uniform or a name tag. You don't work a regular schedule, and you and I are always on the phone. So I'm asking you now. Tell me the truth. What do you do for a living? How can you afford all of the cars, clothes, expensive dinners, jewelry, or even this apartment?"

"Barbie doll," he sighed hesitantly, "I…I don't even know what to say."

"I just want you to tell me the truth. I don't want to make

any assumptions. I want you to tell me exactly what's going on."

"You're so young, baby. You shouldn't have to worry about any of that," he stalled.

"Will, it doesn't matter how young I am. If we're going to be together, you should at least be honest with me about the situation and let me decide if I can handle it. You can't take that right to decide from me," I explained.

"That's true, but…"

"Will, I just saw a white guy stand in front of your door begging you for something on credit even though he had open sores all over his face and arms that looked like they needed a medical investment. Now I'm sincerely trying not to jump to any conclusions. I'd much rather you be up front and honest with me instead of me having to make assumptions," I told him.

"I just don't want you to judge me. That's why I didn't tell you from the very beginning. I wanted you to get to know me first before you counted me out," he told me.

"So my assumptions are right? You're a drug dealer?"

"Barbie doll, I'm not just a drug dealer. I'm one of the biggest crack cocaine, methamphetamine, and heroin manufacturers in the city," he confessed.

"Wait. "Manufacturer'? You MAKE the drugs?" I was shocked.

"Yes, I do. I make some of the highest grade drugs in the state. Some of the biggest dope boys in the city come to me to cook their crack and mix their meth."

I was prepared for Will to say he was selling weed. I could have handled him selling cocaine. I hadn't even considered this aspect of the drug business, let alone think that my boyfriend was a key player in the drug manufacturing business in the city. I didn't even know how to react.

"But you're obviously not cooking this stuff here," I told him. "So where are you making the shit?"

"I have an old house that my grandmother left to my father that he passed down to me. It's about fifty miles outside of town, and it sits in the middle of a few acres of land. It's pretty secluded out there. So a few times a week, I go out there to cook, come back and drop off the finished product and collect my money, and go right back home. Nobody knows where I go. Nobody really even asks me any questions. As long as their product is always A1- and it always is- there really isn't much conversation at all," he explained.

"So you own a whole house and instead of fixing it up and living in it, you've turned it into a meth lab and you're living in an apartment?"

"Yeah. Shit, it's an old house, and it's making me enough money to pay for this apartment and everything else I need."

"You've got to take me out there. I want to see it."

Will looked at me like I was crazy. "No, baby," he said shaking his head. "You can't go out there. It's too dangerous."

"Will, I'm in school for biochemical engineering. I know all of the possible dangers that come with cooking crack," I rolled my eyes at him.

"I'm still not taking you out there, Bre. You're too beautiful to be in a place like that anyway. The dope house is no place for a woman who is wife material."

"What are you hiding out there? You got one of your hos living out there? Is that where you moved Toya to?" I knew what buttons to push and how to push them. I knew Will wasn't going to want to fight this battle with me. He'd much quicker just give up and let me have my way than to even seem as though he was up to something suspicious that involved Toya.

"That shit ain't even funny, Bre. Nobody's living out there. With all of the chemicals and fumes, the place isn't even suitable to serve as living quarters for a dog, let alone a human. And you know I don't fuck with that Toya ho anymore."

"Yeah, well, I assumed that much after she jumped on me, and we see how that turned out," I said sarcastically.

"Bre, don't start that shit," he said as he got up and went back into the kitchen to check the lasagna that was finishing up in the oven.

"Well, why are you acting like there's something to hide out there? If there's nothing to hide, you wouldn't have a problem with me going out there with you just to see what it's like and take a look around," I said, trying to make him feel guilty.

"I'm not acting like anything," he said as he pulled the lasagna out of the oven and turned the oven off. "You're making all of these accusations like that's actually what's going on and it couldn't be further from the truth." He stood in the kitchen doorway and looked at me looking at him with that "prove it" look on my face. "Look, Bre," he sighed in defeat, "if it's really that big of an issue, I'll take you out there with me the next time I go out there so you can see that nobody's out there. There really ain't much of shit out there at all."

"I don't care. I'm going. When are you supposed to go back out there?"

"Sunday to do my weekend orders. I usually head out

there around nine or ten in the morning."

It was just amazing to me how Will had worked out a schedule that even coincided with my school schedule and sleep pattern. Will knew that I usually slept in on Sunday mornings to catch up on any sleep I had missed during the week. He also knew what days and times I had to be in class. It was like he had taken special care to make sure I didn't find out what he was doing.

"I'll be ready," I told him. He huffed and rolled his eyes at me.

"You want Ranch, French, or Italian on your salad?"

Chapter 9

When Sunday morning rolled around, Will was at my door at eight forty-five, making sure I was up and getting dressed.

"Why are you putting on make-up and shit, Bre? You don't have to be a Barbie doll today. There's not going to be anyone out there to see you," he said as he wrapped his arms around me from behind and kissed my neck as I applied eye-shadow in the mirror.

"How many times do I have to tell you that I don't go any-where with you without looking like I belong with you? You never know what might happen or who we may see. You'll never hear anyone asking what you're doing with me. I'm always going to be on point," I explained.

"We're just going there and back. Nobody's going to see us."

"Anything could happen. Lord forbid we end up in a car wreck and I end up unconscious. They're not going to wheel me into the E. R. trying to figure out what I was doing in your car, and if they have to cut my clothes off of me, I bet you my bra and panties will both be clean and they'll match."

"Where do you come up with this stuff?" he laughed at me.

"It's standard woman code," I stated simply as I finished my eyeliner.

"Well, can you get with the board and come up with a shorter standard time limit for getting ready?"

"I'll see what I can do," I giggled. "I'll be ready in just a second, baby."

"Bre, bring your ass on now," he shouted from the living room five minutes later. "I told you ain't nobody gone see you."

"What are you yelling for?" I said quietly from behind him. I was standing there with my purse hanging from my arm, ready to go.

"About time!"

"Nigga, you didn't even have to wait ten minutes. Plus you were early," I said with a slap to his arm. "Now shut your ass up and let's go."

We got to the parking garage and I stood there looking for a car I recognized. Will pressed the button on the remote hanging from his keychain, and the headlights flashed and locked clicked on a dirty light blue Ford Taurus. I just looked at him.

"You coming?" he asked as he opened the passenger door for me.

"Have you lost your mind? Why the hell are we riding in

this piece of shit? Where's the Escalade?"

"C'mon, Bre. Get in," he chuckled while shaking his head. "I'll explain on the way there."

I plopped down on the seat of the Taurus with my lip stuck out, pouting like a baby. I just knew this nigga hadn't put me in a bum ass Ford Taurus like I was average or something. I just stared at the side of his head as he backed out of the parking space and pulled out of the garage.

"What, Bre?" he asked like he didn't know why I was staring at all seven heads he had grown.

"Nigga, you'd better get to explaining real quick why you got me riding in this damn barely-a-car ass hunk of junk. Why aren't we in the Escalade or the Challenger?"

"See, there you go being extra. This is what I always drive when I go out there. It's called a normal car," he joked. "What's wrong with a Taurus?"

"Really? Are you serious right now? Taurus' are ho cars. You don't see anybody but hood hos and baby mommas driving Taurus'. They're disposable cars. They're the cars baby daddies take when their baby mommas piss them off. They go pick up their side bitch; fuck her at a by-the-hour motel; drive around all night making serves, busting donuts, and burning all the rubber off of her tires; and then drop the mother fucker back off with a half a quart of oil and two drops of gas an hour after the kids were supposed to be at school and she was supposed to be at work. They're the cars bitches pile into to go to the club after they've been in the mirror three hours trying to style three packs of five dollar synthetic Yaki and adjusting Walmart bras. They're the cars crackheads ride around in trying to find the dope man and hos ride around in to meet up with their tricks. But it's not the car you drive your college-educated girlfriend around in. I bet you that!"

"Exactly. You just proved my point for me. It's a normal, wholesome, family car. It's under the radar. Everybody knows my truck, and I can guarantee you if we drive down that stretch of highway in the Escalade, the first sheriff or police officer that spots us will have us stretched out on the side of the highway in the dirt stripping the truck down to the frame looking for shit, Plus the Taurus has a decent amount of trunk space to transport shit. You have to remember we have cargo," he explained. I tensed up with the reminder that we were riding with a trunk full of drugs and drug-making supplies.

"Yeah, whatever," I surrendered. "How long does it usually take to get there?"

"A little less than an hour. You're impatient already. We're not even outside of the city limits yet."

"I'm not impatient. I just wanted to know."

"Yeah. Sure. Just relax and enjoy the ride. The ho car, as you call it, is up to date on all of her shots and physicals, so she rides real smooth. She's not pretty, but she's healthy."

I had to admit to myself that Will was right. The Taurus really was a low key car, a perfect decoy. The grey cloth interior wasn't any version of clean, and it was missing two hubcaps, but he had kept up with the maintenance so it ran like a sewing machine.

When we finally pulled into the winding driveway that was almost hidden by the surrounding trees, Will turned the music down.

"Bre, when we go in here, don't touch anything. I don't want you to get any kind of chemicals on your clothes or skin. I've got all kinds of protection in there, like goggles and aprons and masks. I'll give you everything you need, and if you ever need some fresh air, you just step out the back door," he told me.

I simply nodded in agreement as he pulled up in front of a beautiful oak brown two-story house with matching doors and shutters and a porch that wrapped around three sides of it. The house looked to be in good repair, and there were empty flower pots hanging on both sides of the steps, absent of the herbage that had died long ago, probably due to the chemical smoke and lock of love and attention.

Will showed me around the inside of the house. He had moved all of the furniture to the upstairs bedrooms to make a sort of living quarters. The entire first level was a bunch of tables, canisters, and materials to cook the drugs. He had three stoves in the large eat-in kitchen, along with the washer, dryer, dishwasher, and refrigerator.

"So I've given you the initial walk-through," he told me when we made it back to the kitchen. "I've never brought anyone out here, so I've never had to do this before. You're here now, and even if you never come back out here, there are some things I need to show you while you're here today." I was lost and couldn't imagine what else he needed to show me. "Come with me," he said.

I followed him back upstairs and he began with the bedroom. Walking around the bed and standing next to the window, he instructed me to stand next to him.

"We're out in the middle of nowhere, so you never know what might happen. Somebody might be out hunting and stumble upon the house while we're here, and we have to be prepared to defend ourselves. Someone could be watching us, following us, tracking us some kind of way. They come here to ambush us, and we have to be ready with a counter-attack," he told me. "In every single room in this house there is a way to defend yourself," he said while looking into my eyes.

He instructed me to lay on my back on the floor. When he laid next to me, he pointed underneath the bed.

"Underneath the bed, there's a shotgun that's always fully loaded. All the guns are hidden inside the house face north and west. This gun is on a swivel so that you can turn it to aim at whoever is threatening you. You use the bed as your cover and turn the gun on the swivel to aim. Got it?"

There were at least three guns in every room of the house, and they ranged from small handguns with extended clips to AK 47's and AR 15's. There were guns that I knew I couldn't handle and others that I knew I could, guns hidden in plain sight and others obviously hidden. I felt like I was in the middle of a video game, crawling around the floor picking up guns and ammunition.

When we made it back to the kitchen, Will opened the pantry door and handed me goggles, an apron, and gloves. I put them on while he ran to the car to bring the drugs and supplies inside, and once everything was unloaded he began his routine.

"I cook up the crack first," he said as he opened a cabinet next to the window over the kitchen sink. There must have been four dozen boxes of baking soda in that cabinet. "Cooking crack is not like smoking crack. It creates a more normal kind of smoke. When you smoke crack, it creates a very toxic smoke. People who have never been around it tend to feel nauseous and end up with a very sore throat."

"So you've been around people while they were smoking crack?" I asked him as I leaned against the opposite counter.

"When I was younger. You gotta start somewhere. I used to be a small-time dope boy. I was a runner for some of the bigger guys, and I sold weed and sometimes a little crack. Being in the dope house, yes, there were times when I sold a nigga some rocks and he pulled out his pipe and smoked that shit right then and there. When you've got to have it, you've got to have it," he said and shrugged his shoulders.

I watched him measure out cocaine and baking soda with real measuring cups. He was extra careful and very skilled at what he was doing. I could tell that he had been doing it so long that he didn't even really need the measuring cup. He could eyeball it and be accurate or close. Will cut on all of the eyes on the first stove and pulled four identical pots from underneath the counter. With another measuring cup, he added the exact same amount of water to each pot.

"Tell me what you're doing," I told him.

"I didn't know I was supposed to be teaching you how to do this shit. I thought you were just going to watch. Do I need to narrate this like a cooking show?" he laughed.

"Not really. I just wanted to know what you're doing. That's all."

He pulled four contraptions that looked like they were

made from large mason's jars out of another cabinet, poured the baking soda and cocaine mixture into them along with some water, and went to work on the stove. I just watched in silence as he made batch after batch. Cook. Cut. Package. Label. Repeat. A couple of hours later, it was on to the meth.

I watched as Will set up a large contraption that consisted of several smaller gadgets on the kitchen table. He connected pipes, tubing, and random containers, and then went to the cabinets opposite the stove and pulled out jars, containers, and bottles of some of the most random materials.

"What's this stuff?" I asked, pointing at a large jar filled with an odd-looking clear fluid.

"That," he said pointing at the jar, "is the lithium from over a hundred batteries."

"Lithium from batteries?"

"Yeah. I'm going to tell you what everything is and what I'm doing as I go along," he assured me.

I watched in pure shock and amazement as Will mixed and cooked, swirled and cooked, stirred and cooked over a dozen ingredients that were individually hazardous to a person's health to create a drug that I just knew must have been deadly. At one point, we opened all of the doors and windows because the smoke billowing from the substance as it cooked was lethal, even with our masks on. I took mental notes on all of the materials and ingredients and everything Will did.

Will made several batches of meth, each one resulting in an amazingly small amount of finished product when compared to the large amount of effort and materials it took to produce it. Noticing the look on my face, he unwrapped one of the small packages for me to see.

"I know it doesn't look like much, but this little bit right here," he said as he pushed the substance around in the paper, "is actually worth about five hundred dollars." I looked at him and then at the powdery substance in disbelief. "It's dangerous as hell to make, but it's cheap and sells big. All of the ingredients are easily obtainable and most of it is household supply stuff. Acetone, brake fluid, lighter fluid- all normal shit you can grab from just about any store. The meds are about the hardest thing to get because you can only buy so much of it at a time, and they keep it behind the counter at the pharmacy."

"That little bit of dust is worth five hundred dollars? If you sneeze on it, you'll blow the whole batch away."

"I know, but this little bit of nothing gets them high as

hell," he explained.

I was silent the rest of the time we were there. Will watched me watching him as I made mental notations of the ingredients, the process, and the product. I saw Will in an entirely different light. Part of me even admired him because he had already obtained the occupation I was studying so diligently to acquire. I had to admit to myself that as illegal as it was, Will's making and baking was essentially exactly what I wanted to do with my life.

Chapter 10

The next day, Will came over to take me shopping. I had been up most of the night going over what I had seen over and over again in my head.

"Something bothering you, Bre?" he asked while we were in the Challenger.

"No, why?" I tried to play it off.

"You're a lot quieter than usual. Something on your mind?"

"No, I'm good," I lied. Will looked at me out of the corner of his eyes as he drove. I wasn't fooling him a bit.

Will's cousin was throwing a huge party for his birthday at the biggest club in the city, The Mansion. Will saw it as another opportunity to shower me with gifts for passing my finals and to show me off, so we were at the mall to find me a new outfit for the party.

"Bre, just pick one," he fussed as I pondered over three dresses that I just couldn't seem to choose from.

"I can't decide," I whined.

"Look, you can't twerk in this one because it's so tight,

and when you get drunk, this one is going to end up being some sort of wardrobe malfunction," he eliminated two of the choices in seconds.

"Why do you assume I'm going to get drunk or twerk?"

"Because you always do. You sit at the bar and nurse three or four drinks and when they kick in, you get up ready to twerk on this dick."

"Well damn," was all I could say because he was absolutely right.

"Plus, this one matches the Red Bottoms I bought you," he revealed.

"You bought me a pair of Red Bottoms?!" I squealed.

"Yep. They're in the trunk of the car," he smiled as he swiped his card for the dress. "I got something else for you too."

"Really? What is it?"

"C'mon," he said as he handed me the bagged dress. He led me down to the jewelry store. "I'm picking up my order today, Saul," he told the jeweler.

"Of course, Mr. Will. Of course," he said and headed to the back. He returned with a box and set it down on the glass countertop in front of Will. "I made all of the adjustments you requested. It's made to your specifications."

Will opened the box and examined its contents. I stood back, trying not to peek. As anxious as I was, I didn't want to ruin Will's surprise for myself. When he turned around with the box, I looked down into it and gasped. I looked up at Will with my hand over my mouth and tears in my eyes. I guess that was his goal because he was smiling at my reaction.

Will took the chain out of the box and opened the clasp. I turned around and pulled my hair to the side to allow him to put it on me. I examined the charm as it fell against my breasts. Will's charm on his chain was a golden diamond-encrusted money bag with a skull and crossbones that were made from black diamonds. He had the jeweler make a matching charm, b tut with a bottle of Bacardi to the left of the bag and an open tube of lipstick to the right. I had officially become the female version of him.

*   ~   *   ~   *

I don't remember the party that night or any other party that summer. It was all a blur of turning up on Bacardi, twerking on top of tables and counters, Will pulling me down and us fighting in driveways and parking lots, and drunk make-up sex all over both of our apartments, followed by devastating headaches and hangovers. I was getting cursed out weekly by Shaniece, who had settled into the Ivy League life at Princeton and was ready to strangle me for not calling her regularly as I had been. I didn't have time to chit-chat with Shaniece like I usually did. I was too busy enjoying Atlanta's wild nightlife, and she knew it. Her little friends from high school had been calling her about my turn-up sessions at all of the parties in the city. I didn't care. I was living life and loving it.

I rolled over one morning and bumped against Will, startling myself. I must have gotten stupid drunk the night before because I didn't remember how I had gotten home or him coming with me. He was sitting up on his elbow watching me sleep.

"What's wrong, baby?" I said groggily as I frowned and rubbed my eyes.

"Baby, this shit is getting boring," he stated simply with a straight face.

"What?" Truth be told, it was entirely too early in the morning for that shit, and I have never been a morning person. He really was playing with his life starting off first thing in the morning with that bullshit.

"This shit is getting boring, baby. We need to do something new."

"Boring? Nigga, we've been to a different party every night this week. What the hell are you talking about?"

"Partying is cool, but that ain't doing shit. We need to hop on the paper chase."

"Baby, I don't have to work. My parents got me until I graduate and start my career."

"Yeah, but your parents don't got me You and me, baby, we're a winning combination."

"You and me? What do you need me to do?"

"I got a couple of big orders coming through. I trust you, and I've already shown you how to do everything. I need you to help me cook a few times to get this shit done on time."

"You don't want me to help you cook, baby," I chuckled and shook my head. "Believe me."

"Why not?"

"Because I've watched you cook. I'd upgrade your shit to such a high quality your customers would get twice the high from half the product."

"See, that's the kind of thinking I'm talking about, the kind of player I need on my team. You're going to school for this chemical shit. You know all about the right combination of compounds and balancing chemical equations. I mean, my shit is already top of the line high grade. With you as head chef, I'd be able to provide hybrid dope. Shit that the game ain't never seen before. And they'll only be able to get it from me. I'll have a monopoly on these streets," he explained.

I turned his words over in my head. He was right, of course, but I had to consider the risks I was taking becoming involved in is criminal activity. Up until this point I had kept my hands clean and hadn't done anything illegal except getting wasted underage. I'd be taking a huge chance, but, I decided, it was worth it for my man.

"Okay," I said quietly, still not quite sure. "I'll do it, but I have to stay in the shadows. I don't want any of the recognition or attention. Nobody can know that I'm involved in this. I've got too much to lose."

"That's the plan, Barbie doll. I wouldn't put you at risk, baby. I'm going to take care of you and keep you out of harm's way," he assured me.

"So when do you need me to start?"

"Now."

The first time I helped Will cook, it took us an hour to start on the first batch because I came into the kitchen and completely rearranged his equipment and contraptions to create a smoother and more precise process. I had brought some higher grade and name-brand materials, scales, and measuring equipment. Of course, Will didn't completely understand, but he trusted my expertise. So he cooked the crack- this time with a higher-grade Arm & Hammer baking soda mixed with a few of my extra ingredients- while I concocted a hybrid form of meth that almost could have been considered its own type of drug. There was less smoke, but it was definitely more toxic, so we opened all the windows and, at one point, the front door.

Will's first time selling it, people were a little skeptical because the color of it was just a little off. But when they hit that shit, they were hooked. The dope boys he was selling it to were calling him left and right, trying to get more of it to satisfy their customers' sudden high demand. When we saw what a success it was, Will raised the price of the new product by twenty percent.

I started cooking for Will all day every Saturday and Sunday, partying on Sunday nights, and then cooking again after class three days a week. Somewhere in between, Will found the time to ease up my skirt or bend me over the kitchen counter, and we were satisfied just like that.

When I started taking more advanced chemistry classes, I took everything I learned in class and in the lab and implemented it all during our cooking sessions. New ingredients, additional equipment, more efficient methods- Will would look at me like I was crazy every single time and then be amazed at how much of an improvement he saw in the results. I'm not sure what I had created out in those backwoods, but the final product was such an improvement from the original recipe that it definitely was a completely different drug.

Word spread fast about the new, improved drug. All of the drug dealers were asking Will what he was doing differently, and, of course, he didn't tell them. How could he? I was the one mixing the new batches and he had no idea what the new recipe consisted of. I even encouraged him to take all of the credit for the new product so that everyone was unaware that I was even remotely involved. If you asked anyone else, I was still completely oblivious to Will's criminal activity.

Eventually, Will and I ventured into the heroin business as well. I was damn near a full-time chef in the kitchen. We had expanded our lab area throughout the entire first floor of the house and set up multiple stations. We had specific methods in place to keep the products separated when we were cooking multiple drugs or products for multiple dealers, which was almost always the case. I had started doing most of the shopping for the newer ingredients, and I had even started clipping coupons for items such as Drano and batteries to help increase our profits.

Chapter 11

"So this is what we're doing now?"

"Huh?" I moaned groggily.

"You heard me. So this is what we're doing now, Bre? I go from talking to you every day to not hearing from you in almost six months and I'm supposed to be okay with that?"

"I've been busy with school and shit. My bad."

"Your bad? Bre, it ain't that much studying in the damn world. So you're lying to me too now, huh?"

"Lying about what, Chloe? I've been busy with school. Where's the lie in that?" Yet again, it was too early in the morning for a mother fucker to be fucking with me.

"Right there falling off of your lips. That's where it's at. I'm not stupid, Bre, and I'm not deaf either. I've heard all about your partying and shit. Hell, Shaniece and I go to the same school. Her little friends call her telling her all of these crazy stories about what the fuck you've been doing down there, and she comes straight to me telling me all about your new adventure. I don't give a fuck about you table dancing and shaking your ass. I want to know who the nigga is."

"Nigga? What nigga?"

"Bre, why must you talk to me like I'm dumb? All the partying and shit is normal for somebody who just got their freedom papers, but you didn't come home for the holidays, and you didn't come home during the summer either. You can act like you don't know what the fuck I'm talking about, but I'm not slow. Ain't shit but a good piece of dick going to make you keep your ass in Atlanta all that time when you know your parents want to see you."

I thought about what she said. She actually was right. I had been so caught up with Will and our hustle that I hadn't realized I had allowed over a year to pass since I had seen my parents. I could only imagine their disappointment when I hadn't returned home for Christmas.

"I talk to my parents all the time, Chloe. They understand," I tried to make an excuse for myself.

"Believe me, I'm sure they understand. But they're not blinded by your lies either. They were young once. I'm sure your mother remembers what it was like when she first met your father. I'm sure your father remembers chasing after your mother. You've got your first taste of freedom, so I know they've caught a hint of what's really going on."

"Well, I'm sorry to disappoint you all, but I've simply been caught up with my academic life," I lied.

"Bitch, you go to Georgia Tech! You don't have an academic life! I go to Princeton and still have time to visit my mother during the holidays and call my dad on his birthday. So since you're so caught up with your academic life, I expect you to bring your academic life home with you for the holidays so we can see just how caught up you've been."

"But, Chloe, I told you-"

"Oh, I heard the lie the first time you told it. I ain't stupid. You just make sure you bring the nigga home with you when you come for Christmas this year because you WILL be coming home for the holidays," she demanded. "You got that?"

"Yeah, Chloe. I got it," I surrendered.

"Good. I'll talk to you later. Bye." Click. I just looked at the phone. Typical Chloe. Hit and run. More like sock a punch and run.

*   ~   *   ~   *

It took serious persuading, but I finally convinced Will to go home to Memphis with me for the holidays to present ourselves as a couple. When my mother found out we were coming, she went completely overboard decorating, ordering, planning, and cooking. I knew my mother. She was a perfectionist and an enthusiast. She always went above and beyond to make sure every holiday season was the definition of merry and bright.

The problem was I knew what they were expecting: a young, distinguished, mild-mannered college student who came from a wealthy or at least middle-class family and who had potential and aspirations to obtain a well-paying career in a respectable profession. It wasn't that Will didn't have enough home training; he knew how to be respectful and polite. It wasn't that he didn't have goals and dreams because he definitely did. He just wasn't focused on doing anything better because he was having such great success at what he was involved in at the present moment. As far as outward appearance, I knew my mother would have a heart attack and my father would likely threaten to kill us both. Everything about the way he looked screamed "Stay away!" especially for an innocent minded, sheltered, rich little-spoiled brat like me. The gold teeth, the dreadlocks, the tattoos, his style of dress… my parents were going to be mortified, and I knew it.

We drove my car home the week before Christmas with plans to stay about a week and then return to Atlanta before New Year's Eve to make it to Will's friend's New Year's Eve party at The Mansion. As I pulled into the winding driveway at my parents' house, I saw my parents standing there waiting with Chloe, Shaniece, Aunt Sharon, and Tristian. Everything in me was telling me to just turn around and go on back to Atlanta. Within about five seconds, everything that could have possibly gone wrong flashed through my head. Instead of following my instinct though, I pulled up to the house.

Before we got out, I looked at Will and said, "Baby, no matter what, just remember that I love you."

"I know, baby," he said as he grabbed my hand. "Everything will be okay. Don't worry." He winked at me, I smiled, and we got out together.

Everyone's facial expressions changed and Chloe's jaw dropped when they looked at Will, and then they immediately caught themselves and forced smiles back onto their faces.

"Oh, Bre. Hey, baby," my mother said as she smiled and

hugged me.

"Hey, Momma. Daddy," I said as I hugged them both. "Mom and Dad, this is Will, my boyfriend," I introduced them.

"Hello, William," my father said as he offered his hand.

"How are you, Mr. Braxton?" Will said with a distinguished voice and shook my father's hand with a firm grip.

"I'm well, and yourself?"

"I'm blessed," he answered. I swallowed laughter at the inside joke. Lord knows he was. "And Mrs. Braxton, hello. How are you?"

"I'm just fine, William," she said while staring directly at his teeth. "Ummm, this is my sister, Sharon, and her daughter Shaniece," she introduced them.

"Yes, yes. Shaniece and I have met. How are you?" he asked Shaniece.

"I'm fine, Will," she smiled in amusement, fighting back her own laughter.

"Nice to meet you, Ms. Sharon," Will said as he gently shook my aunt's hand as well.

"Delighted," Aunt Sharon said simply, doing a horrible job at hiding her disgust.

"Will, this is Chloe, my best friend," I said.

"It's great to finally put a face with the name," Chloe said. "I've heard so much about you. She talks about you all the time," she lied.

"It's great to meet you too. The pleasure is all mine."

"And, Will, this is Tristian. He's a great friend of mine, and he lives just a couple of streets over," I said, trying to sugar coat the friendship.

"Hey, how are you doing, man?" Tristian said in the most monotonous, unenthusiastic tone I had ever heard scratch its way out of his throat.

"I'm great. How are you?" Will smiled politely.

"I'm cool," Tristian said as he ran his hand over his crew cut and then straightened his Ralph Lauren button down. I just glared at Tristian, unable to believe that he was being so blatantly rude. He glared back at me, attempting to send a message with his ocean blue eyes, but I couldn't decipher exactly what it was.

"Why don't we all go into the house?" my mother interrupted the awkwardness of the moment.

"Great idea," my father agreed and then ushered us all into the house. Will grabbed my hand, catching me off guard, and then glanced down at me with a smile.

My mother showed us all to the living room where she

had small finger foods laid out. Everyone made small talk as my mother and my aunt finished dinner while discussing our guest, I was sure.

I ran to my room to grab a photo album Chloe had mentioned during the conversation, and on the way back, I bumped into Tristian who was coming out of the downstairs bathroom.

"Bre, can I talk to you for a second?" he pulled me to the side.

"Sure. What's up?" I asked.

"Bre, is this…is this what we've come to?"

"What do you mean, Tristian?" I asked him, confused.

"I mean, Bre, I know we never saw eye to eye much after I started smoking weed. I know that was the reason you kind of pulled away from me, but, honestly, Bre! You leave for school at a college that is not worthy of a student of your caliber. You don't call me or Chloe anymore. You don't come home. And then the first time you come home in over a year, you bring this guy?" he scoffed.

"What's that supposed to mean?" I frowned, offended.

"First of all, I know I got deep into the weed and shit, but this guy looks like he does a lot more than just kush."

"He does not!" I gasped at his insinuation.

"If you say so, but if you ask me, judging by his height and size, he's probably pretty acquainted with the coca leaves."

"He does not do cocaine, Tristian!" I whispered furiously.

"Even if he doesn't, Bre, look at him. I don't care what kind of packaging you put on a pitbull. It's still a pit bull. You can wash it up, put a pretty collar on it, even dress it up with the cute little puppy outfits. Under all of that, there's still a much larger, much meaner, and much more vicious dog than the poodle you tried to dress it up as, and when he growls, you'll still see his teeth."

"What the fuck is that supposed to mean, Tristian?"

"You can put the khakis and the button down on this guy, but he's still a thug, Bre. Underneath the Tommy Hilfiger or Nautica he has on, he's still a thug, a gangster, a common hoodlum…and he's no good for you," he said bluntly.

"Who are you to tell me what is or isn't good for me? Huh? Was all of that weed you were offering me good for me" I retorted. "That man hasn't done anything wrong. If anyone isn't good for me, it's you. You stand here all high and mighty being judgmental, judging a man by his outward appearance while you have the opportunity to get to know who he really is and you're dismissing it."

"I don't need to get to know him to know that nothing good is going to come from this," he whispered calmly. "You'd better just hope that I and the rest of your family and friends are still around to put the pieces of your broken heart back together when he throws it against the wall and watches it shatter."

"Yeah, well, if he does, whether you're around or not, I'll be just fine," I snarled. I saw the sting of my words in his eyes, though he put forth a commendable attempt to conceal it. I returned to the living room and Tristian waited a few moments and then re-entered the room as well.

The tension between Tristian and I was thick during dinner, and his disapproving glare made it very obvious. Everyone pummeled Will with questions about his upbringing, life in Atlanta, and his future goals, which he was all too willing to answer with responses that I could tell were prewritten but did sound genuine when he offered them. Tristian was eerily quiet for quite a while, but when he finally spoke, the entire conversation shifted.

"So, Will, where did you meet Bre'ana?" he asked and then shoved a forkful of pot roast in his mouth, staring at Will the entire time.

"We met at a party when Bre'ana was in town for the summer a few years ago." Will knew exactly what he was doing. Tristian thought we had just met since I had been in school there. He had one up on Tristian.

"Really?" Tristian raised an eyebrow at the news. "So you've been dating all of this time?"

"Yes, we have," I smiled widely.

"Were you aware of this, Mr. Braxton?" Tristian turned to

my father who had only been making simple comments and polite remarks up until this point.

"No," my father said nonchalantly. "I was unaware that Bre'ana had been dating anyone. He must be a pretty awesome young man, huh, Tristian?"

"I'm not sure I follow you, sir. Bre'ana's been hiding her relationship with him for a number of years. That level of deceit doesn't qualify him as awesome in my opinion," Tristian challenged.

"On the contrary, Tristian. The fact that Bre'ana was able to maintain a relationship with William while they lived hundreds of miles apart for a number of years shows the young man's loyalty to my daughter. Also, I might note that they've been involved all of this time and Bre'ana's grades have not wavered even a bit. He hasn't interfered with her education at all, so therefore, he must also be pretty understanding, and perhaps even encouraging."

"But, sir, they've been essentially lying to you both for years. You can't honestly believe that's worthy of your approval," Tristian was confused and angry that his plan had backfired.

"Yes, yes. This is true," my father nodded. "But you will learn throughout the years, Tristian, that a woman's heart is a deep ocean of secrets." He nodded and winked at him and then continued eating.

"Titanic," Chloe mumbled.

"What?" Tristian asked, aggravated.

"It was a quote from Titanic," she told him.

It seemed my father had shut down the conversation. Tristian sat quietly pouting like a spanked puppy, likely concocting ways to throw shade on my relationship with Will as the rest of us discussed school and work like normal adults. I could tell Will was amused by Tristian's little display of manhood. I guess he was pretty secure at that point that I was not going to leave him and no one's opinion of him or our relationship mattered to me.

"Well, William, you certainly do make a good first impression, young man," my father smiled at him.

"Ha!" Tristian laughed before Will could even swallow his food to say thank you. Everyone turned and looked at him. "He's hardly a man," he laughed. My mother gasped at the rude insult.

"Tristian, mind your manners," she told him.

"Look at him. He's not accustomed to manners anyway. He doesn't know the difference."

"And even if that were true, that would still be no reason to treat him as if he were beneath you. You will not sit at our table and treat our guest as if he were less than," my father warned him.

"It's okay, Mr. Braxton," Will spoke up. "I'd actually be interested in hearing Tristian's evaluation and opinion of me since he seems to be so insistent upon voicing it. If nothing else, I'm sure I'll find it entertaining."

"You want my opinion of you?" Tristian asked with narrowed eyes. "You think it'd be entertaining? I dare not argue with a guy who doesn't know the difference between his salad fork and his dessert fork at the dinner table," he threw shade.

"I'm not sure if you're jealous because Bre'ana is dating me or intimidated because you know I'm twice the man that you are," Will said and glanced down at his lap with a dramatic pause, "but either way, your antics don't impress me and your insults don't offend me. You can sit here and say whatever you want, but you know nothing about me, and that's what bothers you the most. Here you are, an Ivy League student who's been knowing Bre'ana for years. I come into the picture and sweep the woman that you were so sure was yours off of her feet, and you can't stand to lose the battle. So you can throw all of these verbal shots, but unless you're ready to square up, you'll find me unbothered and uninterested." With that, Will took a sip from his glass and then placed his hand on top of mine on the table.

"Is that a threat?" Tristian fumed.

"Honestly, it sounds more like a challenge to me," my father clarified.

"I'm not going to fight you like one of your homies," Tristian scoffed.

"Scared?" my father asked.

123

"Terrified," I laughed.

"I am not! Look!" He stood up with his finger pointed at my nose. "I've been right around the corner all your life. I know you like I know the time's tables. You take one little summer vacation in Georgia and throw everything we've built away."

"What have we built, Tristian? We have never been a couple, never hugged, never kissed. You blew any chance you would have had years ago," I stood up to see eye to eye with him.

"For heaven's sake, that doesn't mean sink to this low! You could have at least done better than me! You come home with a nigger! He's a straight up nigger!" he shouted.

Every single person at the dinner table gasped and every tongue fell silent. There was a loud resounding silence that was almost deafening, followed by the sound of Will's chair on the floor. I instantly grabbed him, wrapped my arms around his neck, and kissed his lips gently. He looked into my eyes and I saw the rage begin to melt away. I couldn't tell if Tristian just expected everyone to be cool about what he had said or if he had forgotten that he was the only white person in the house, but what was very clear was that Will was ready to squeeze his neck until his eyes bulged out of their sockets.

"Tristian, you are excused from my dinner table, and I'm going to have to ask you to leave my house," my mother said in shock.

"But, Mrs. Braxton-"

"Now!" my father yelled. "Get your ass up, boy, and get out of my house. And don't you bring your ass back around here. If I ever, if I ever see you here again, you die. Just like that," he snapped his fingers.

Chloe laughed and said, "Carlito's Way."

Tristian tossed his napkin onto the table, rose from his chair, and stormed out of the house.

"William, honey, I am so sorry," my mother offered an apology.

"No need to apologize, Mrs. Braxton. The ignorance of one, in my eyes, will never be able to misrepresent the many," he said.

"Mom, Dad, I think we're going to go ahead and head back to Atlanta," I told them.

"Are you sure, sweetie? You don't have to go." My mother's disappointment was evident in her eyes.

"Baby, I'm okay. We don't have to go. We can just go to the hotel and start fresh tomorrow," Will offered.

"When we start fresh tomorrow, we're heading back home," I told him. "You don't deserve this. This is a bit much. This is crazy."

"Well, before you leave, can I have a few minutes with my baby girl?" my father asked.

"Of course, Daddy," I smiled. I kissed Will's cheek, gave him a reassuring smile, and then followed my father to his office.

"Thank you for standing up for Will, Daddy," I said as he closed the door behind us. "I can't believe Tristian acted like that. It's so embarrassing."

"Well, sweetie, as extremely ill-mannered as he may have been, he wasn't wrong," he said frankly, catching me off guard.

"What?" What do you mean?"

"Sweetie, I'm sure William is a great guy and judging by the smile on your face when you look at him, I'm sure he treats you right," he assured me, "but, honey, he's not even in the same league that you're in. You deserve better, sweetie."

"Better? What could be better than a man who loves me? A man who thinks the world of me?" I whined.

"A man who loves you, thinks the world of you, and can afford you and the lifestyle you're accustomed to living," he stated. Seeing the look on my face, he said, "Listen, Bre'ana. I know you probably have fallen in love with him, and I can only imagine- though I'd rather not think about it- what kind of physical level the two of you have gone to. But, sweetie, there are other fish in the sea. Much larger, faster swimming, prize fish that can feed you a whole lot longer, baby girl."

"Why do I need a rich man, Daddy? I don't have to have a rich man. And Will has money! Just because he has gold teeth and tattoos doesn't mean he doesn't have money."

"I'm sure he does, sweetie. I just pray that his income is of legal means. Look, Bre'ana, I'm not telling you what to do. This is your life and your decision, and I'm a huge advocate for allowing you young kids to make your own mistakes. If he breaks your heart in the end, I'll be here to console you. If he marries you, I'll be here to walk you down the aisle. All I ask is that you be careful, sweetie. Watch him and watch your surroundings. Don't let this guy take you down through the trenches. You're worth so much more than that."

"Knock, knock!" came my mother's voice as she poked her head in the door. "How are things going in here?"

"Mom, Dad is giving me a speech about not letting Will hurt me and how I deserve better."

"Well, Bre'ana, your father's right. I'm sure Will is a nice boy, but, sweetheart, he's not the one for you," my mother said.

"Mom," I gasped.

"No, Bre'ana," she shook her head. "He's out of his league with you and I'm sure you have no idea just what you're getting into. I'm sure everything is all sunshine and roses right now, but this guy has the potential to do you more harm than good, and I just refuse to allow you to do that to yourself."

"What are you saying?"

"I'm saying you have to stop seeing him."

"No!"

"Yes, you have to, Bre'ana. There will be other guys. Guys who are much better for you and can take care of you. You'll get over him and you'll find someone more suitable."

"You can't make me stop seeing him. Daddy, tell her she can't make me!"

"It's true. She can't make you. But you must respect your mother, Bre'ana," he said.

"I'm not going to stop seeing him," I said, arms folded across my chest. I was pouting like a baby.

"If you refuse, I'm going to cut you off, Bre'ana," my mother said with a straight face.

"Cut me off?"

"Yes," she nodded. "You're going to turn over your credit cards and when your lease is up, it will be up to you to renew it or vacate the apartment."

"Daddy, are you seriously going to stand here and let her do this?" I looked at him with tears in my eyes.

"Even though she did not discuss this with me, I'm in no

position to argue. What your mother says goes, Bre'ana,"
he stated. I looked back and forth between the two of them,
unable to believe what I was hearing.

"Seriously?" I said. They both stood there unmoved. "Fine
then," I said, and exited the office. I snatched my purse from
the rack by the door, pulled all three cards out of my billfold,
and slapped them into my mother's open hand. "C'mon, Will.
Let's go," I said as I grabbed his hand with my eyes locked
with my mother's.

"Baby-" he started, but I cut him off.

"Just come on," I said to him quietly, sucking back in the
tears that foolishly thought I would allow them to fall. Will
exited the door, and I stormed out behind him, making sure to
slam the door behind myself. I handed Will the car keys. He
opened my door for me and then hopped into the driver's seat.

Chapter 12

"Bre'ana, what's wrong? What happened?" he asked as he drove to the hotel.

"Just take me to the hotel, Will. I just need a minute. I'm okay," I said quietly as I stared out the window, unable to believe what had just happened.

I had never known my father to back down to my mother and allow her to do anything he disagreed with. I had no clue what was going on between them, but I knew my father well enough to know what he didn't agree with what my mother had just done. It didn't matter, though. He had done nothing to stop her. I was on my own now and had no plans to find myself back in the presence of my parents any time soon.

"I'm going to run us a bath," Will said as we walked into our hotel room. "Hopefully the hot water will help to relax you some."

I plopped down on the edge of the bed and exhaled deeply. All I could think about was what the fuck I was going to do. I kept telling myself not to even worry about it because I knew I'd be straight. My mind just didn't work like that. I had never ventured from underneath my parents' financial wings, and the world I was entering was filled with uncertainty.

Laying back on the bed, I watched Will going back and

forth between our bags and the bathroom as he prepared the tub. One thing I loved about Will was that he understood me. He knew he didn't have to push me to give him information. If he just gave me a moment, I'd always tell him what was going on.

The last time he went into the bathroom, I decided to go ahead and get up and get undressed so I'd be ready when the tub was filled. I stood in the full mirror on the closet door admiring my body. I had developed beautiful curves since I had started college, which I was sure I could thank Will for. My hips had spread. My thighs were thicker. My breasts were fuller.

Will came out of the bathroom completely naked and stood behind me in the mirror. I stared at the two of us as he wrapped his arms around me from behind, kissed my neck and cheek, and admired us in the mirror with his chin in my shoulder. We were a beautiful couple. His milk chocolate skin against my mocha was a beautiful combination. The look of his muscles against my breasts was sexy.

"The water's ready, Wifey," he whispered in my ear.

I turned around to face him, took his cheek in my palm, and kissed him gently. Placing one hand at the small of my back, he kissed me back as he pulled me close and then walked me into the bathroom.

I laid there with my eyes close, my back against his chest, his heart beating against my spine. It felt like I was exactly where I was supposed to be. I was at peace, comfortable, calm, right there with the man I loved. We didn't speak for about twenty minutes. We just sat in silence and enjoyed the feel of our skin pressed against each other until I finally decided I should speak up and tell him what happened.

"My parents cut me off today," I said quietly.

"Cut you off? Why? Were you spending too much money?"

"They cut me off because I refused to stop dating you," I said as I looked over my shoulder into his eyes.

"What?" he exhaled. "I thought they liked me."

"They did. They actually did. They just feel like I can do better. They wanted me to find a man with money, and no gold teeth…and fewer tattoos," I giggled.

"Bre, I can't let you walk away from your family for me. You've had your parents all your life. You've never been on your own. I don't want to come between you and your parents. I'd never make you choose," he said.

"Will…" I took a second to gather my thoughts. "Baby, I know you'd never make me choose, but I've already made my choice. I'd rather do it on my own and live freely than to have the crutch of their help and be under their thumb, chained to their opinions, oppressed by their rules. I've listened to them and followed their rules all my life, but one thing I refuse to allow them to do is to tell me who I can and cannot love."

"But, baby, you've never been on your own. It ain't easy

out here on your own."

"I'm not by myself. I have you."

"You'll always have me. I'll always be here for you," he assured me.

"I know," I smiled. "And you're all I'll ever need, baby. You and I- we're a winning combination. We can't lose."

"Everybody has the ability to lose. Don't use the word 'can't' because we definitely could. But we won't. We'll refuse to lose. And with that always in mind, we'll win," he told me.

"We won't lose," I said.

"Right," he said and kissed my forehead. "So how are we going to do this? I mean, we make damned good money cooking for the dope boys. We can live off of that. No doubt. But we aren't going to want to do that forever, are we?"

"Of course not. We'll keep cooking for right now. When something better comes along, we'll get out of the business. I've only got a couple of years left in school. When I graduate and get a good job offer, we'll be set."

"That's cool for you, but what about me? I don't want to live off of you. We're a team. We'll always be a team. I've got to pull my weight too."

"I'm sure it won't be too hard to figure something out for you, baby. I can take care of us until you get on your feet.

That's a distance down the road, though. We'll develop a solution once the problem is in hand," I told him.

"Bre, you don't have to do this. You shouldn't have to struggle because of me."

"Ssshhh," I pressed my finger to his lips. "I love you, Will. Wherever you are is where I'll be because without you there is no me." I kissed him deeply as I turned around to straddle him in the tub.

"Bre, you're crazy, but I love you too. No woman in their right mind would do what you've decided to do just because you love me. And just because you love me that much, I'm going to make sure I take care of you at all costs. If anything happens to you, it has to happen to me first," he promised me.

"Oh, Will," I whispered and then kissed him again as I gently moved his rock-hard dick into position and slid down on it.

There was always something so relaxing about having Will's dick inside of me. It felt like the stars just aligned in the sky every time he entered my womb, and everything became right with the world. A symphony played every single time we made love. Every stroke was a bow against the strings of a violin. Every gentle touch or caress was a blow into a flute. It consoled all of my woes and comforted my heart.

Will's hands palmed my ass as my hips rocked back and forth on his hard rod. I watched the emotions as they changed on his face, loving his reactions. His eyes closed as I rolled my hips and planted kisses down his cheek. Somewhere along the way, I had missed the changes in Will's body. He had gained weight and built muscles. He arms were stronger, more masculine, and his chest was more muscular. He had abs now and a V where his thighs met his hips. I loved the way he looked before, but I loved the new look even more. His muscles turned me on. Even if I hadn't been sitting in a tub of water, I still would've been soaking wet.

He lifted my nipple to his lips and licked in a circular motion around it before engulfing it between his lips. I moaned and grinded down hard on his dick, making it touch the bottom of my womb. His grunt was so sexy to me. Just knowing that I pleased him made me want him even more. He released my nipple from the grip of his lips, and as he looked up into my eyes to witness the pleasure hidden within, his lips pressed against mine and then consumed them. I became lost in the passion, tumbling in a whirlwind of emotions and sensations.

Will held my hips and directed my motions, ever-aware that I was still learning, but I didn't need much direction. My emotions had sent my hormones into a tropical storm which had caused my body to react on its own. The only thought that was running through my mind was how much I loved him. I instinctively treated the moment like it would be our last. My parents trying to tear us apart had made every second I spent with Will that much more precious. Every stroke felt that much deeper, every kiss that much sweeter. There was something so liberating about giving my parents those credit cards back. I felt free. I could breathe. It was like my first breath of fresh air after I had been drowning under water. I never intended to dive again.

"Let me teach you how to surfboard," he whispered into my neck.

"Like Beyoncé in "Drunk In Love"?"

"Yep. Can you turn around on it without taking it out?"

"I think so," I said and took my time turning around, being careful not to come off of it.

"Now relax some. I'm going to lift you up some and move your feet into position. Hold on to the side of the tub," he instructed and then slid his hands underneath my ass and lifted me up. I held my position where he stopped and he moved my legs so that my feet were flat. "Now, you're going to rock like you're riding a wave on a surfboard."

My mind was telling me I couldn't do it, but the more I rocked, the more comfortable I became. The more comfortable I became, the more confident I became. The more confident I became, the harder I grinded down on it until Will was hitting what I knew must have been the bottom of my womb and the top of some organ that had never been touched.

"That's it, baby," he moaned as I closed my eyes and zoned out. I wasn't even facing him, but I could see Will's face in my mind. His lips, his eyes, his hair. His hands reached out for me and gently caressed my cheek. His lips kissed me tenderly. He was my every thought, my every breath, my every heartbeat, my everything.

Thoughts of our past flashed through my mind. The night we met played in my head, followed by Shaniece questioning me the morning after. I saw myself smiling while sitting by the pool at Shaniece's house talking to him on the phone, blushing when approached by him in the mall, giddy when he pulled into Shaniece's driveway to pick me up. The night Toya attacked me flashed, but was quickly shoved out of the way by the memory of the first time Will and I made love.

I heard myself cry out in the distant reality and felt real tears run down my cheeks.

"Don't cry, baby," he whispered to me. "It's going to be just fine, baby."

"Oh, Will!" I yelled. "Oh shit, Will!"

"Are you about to nut for me, baby? Nut hard on this dick, Barbie doll," he said as he caressed my breasts.

"Baby, I'm finna…ugh…ugh…ahh," I moaned as I bounced.

"Nut hard for me, baby. Give me all of it. All of it, baby," he whispered with his lips against the back of my neck. The wind of his breath sent chills up my spine and pushed me over the edge. My hands squeezed the sides of the tub so tight my knuckles turned white. A burning flame shot from my toes to my nose and the chills in my spine turned into quivers and shivers.

"Will! Will! Willllllllllll!" I cried out as I experienced the most extreme orgasm I had ever felt.

"That's my baby," Will said as he wrapped his arms

around my waist and lifted me with him as he stood up. Standing me on my feet by the sink, he said quietly, "Bend that ass over."

"In the bathroom, baby?"

"Hell yeah!"

I raised an eyebrow at him. We had never done it standing up, let alone with me bent over a sink. I grabbed the edge of the sink and bent over with an arch in my back just like Will liked. Gripping my hip with his left hand, he guided himself back inside of me with his right. Then, with both hands holding on tight to my waist, slid the entire length of his dick inside of me. I gasped as I felt the head of his eight inches touch the bottom of my womb, knowing it was going to be sore in the morning from him beating it up.

Will long stroked me slow and deep as I watched our reflection in the vanity mirror. His eyes were closed and his head thrown back. He sped up his stroke gradually until he was pounding me with the force of a beast, killing the pussy. Curiosity got the best of me, and I looked up into the mirror to see what kind of faces I was making. Beads of sweat were forming on Will's forehead and my eyes were glossed over. Will grabbed the back of my head with an open palm and pulled my hair.

"I love you, Bre. I want you to understand that. You hear me? I love you, girl," he huffed as he pumped deep inside of me.

"I love you too, baby," I moaned.

"Say that shit, girl," he growled.

"I love you, baby!"

"Say it again. What's my name?"

"Will! I love you, Will!"

"That's what I'm talking about. Now nut hard for me on this dick. Throw that ass back."

I twerked on it as I threw it back and read the pleasure on Will's face like a book in the mirror. I couldn't take it and neither could he. His eyes closed and then mine closed too and I creamed all over his joystick. Will suddenly yanked it out and sprayed his kids all over my ass.

Breathing heavily in exhaustion, I moved to get up but was forced back down by Will's palm pressed flat against my spine.

"Don't move, baby. Let me clean you up."

He reached around me and turned on the faucet. Wetting a clean towel with warm water, he gently wiped each and every drop off of my ass and then proceeded to bend down and place wet, gentle kisses all over my ass. It tickled and I giggled. When he stood up, he turned me around, wrapped his arms around me, and kissed me deeply.

I slept on his chest that night, comforted by his presence, content with my life. Pleasing my parents no longer mattered to me. The only thing that mattered was me, myself, and I.

Will didn't even matter. He was content just having me by his side. He didn't require anything from me but my presence and attention, and he was going to get that anyway because I loved him. As he held me close to him, I knew everything would be just fine, and the man I loved was going to make sure of that.

Chapter 13

Will and I went back to Atlanta the next morning. There was nothing left for me in Memphis. I loved my parents, but they had made their opinions and positions clear, so I decided to just love them from a distance. During the drive back home, Will and I had a serious talk about our future together. We decided that Will should move in with me to save us money as a couple since I had suddenly become a liberated woman and would be responsible for my own bills. I was going to keep going to school and keep cooking with Will and eventually we would get out of the business.

We hadn't put up a Christmas tree before we left because we intended to spend the holidays with my family, but since we had a change of plans, I bought a tree and a ridiculous amount of decorations and while Will was out one evening finishing up packing at his apartment, I decorated the entire apartment by myself.

Will came through the door that evening with his arms full of boxes and a bunch of bags hanging from his shoulders. When he saw what I had done- the Christmas tree aglow, the scent of apples and cinnamon in the air, the garland trimming the doorways- he dropped all of his luggage and scooped me up in his arms to kiss me. The least I could do was make him feel at home and welcome in the house we now shared.

"Baby, I know I said I wanted to go to the party for New

Year's Eve, but how about we turn up at home instead?" he asked me after we made love after dinner that night. "We can buy some liquor and snacks, put on some music, and have our own private party right here in the living room. There's no point of us going out getting, bumped around in the middle of a crowd, and having to fight traffic to get back home. We can avoid all of that by staying here."

The idea did sound enticing. I had gotten used to going to parties as a way to spend time with Will, but it was noticeable that he wasn't the party animal that he used to be. He was much more focused on the paper chase than the turn-up.

"If you really want to we can stay home, but we don't have to," I told him.

"I'd much rather be here with you, Barbie doll."

"Well, if we're going to stay home, we've got to find something to make it fun," I suggested.

"Nah, see. That's your job. You see all of these beautiful decorations you've put up? You're good at this kind of shit. You put together the fun part and I'll just play along," he said as he stroked my hair.

"No matter what it is?"

"Anything at all, baby. Standard rules apply, of course. If it's anything sexual, you ain't playing with my ass. We aren't wasting good food, and nothing that's going to require extensive cleanup efforts," he instructed.

"Define extensive," I challenged him.

"Bre, I'm not about to play with you," he chuckled. "Seriously though, only a mess that we can clean up ourselves. Nothing that would deem the apartment unrecognizable."

Will had deliveries to make all day on New Year's Eve. When he left that morning, I gave him a duffel bag and told him to change clothes before he came home for the party. I spend most of the day putting up streamers and other decorations while cooking Rotel, chicken wings, and homemade pizza. Closer to time for Will to arrive, I set out shrimp cocktails and salmon dip and then rushed to change clothes and doll myself up. The moment I heard Will's car alarm's distinctive beep, I readied myself.

The look on Will's face when he opened the door said it all. The decorations, the colorful lights, the food, the liquor, and to top it off my ass bouncing in some pink booty shorts and cropped tank top on a pole I had installed in the middle of the living room. It was over. He closed the door, sat his duffel bag of money on the floor next to the sofa, and then pressed his dick against my bouncing ass.

I threw that ass in a circle and then did the fuck it challenge all on his dick. I pushed him down on the sofa so that he could watch the dance I had choreographed for him. I had taken ballet classes most of my life, so I was light on my feet and I had been practicing on the pole after school while he was out making deliveries.

I climbed to the top of the pole and spun around it once. Then I flipped upside down and twerked as I slid down slowly. I relished in the look of amazement on Will's face. Coming down into a handstand, I made my ass clap and then fell into a split. Up and down the pole I went. Upside down, right side up, one hand, both hands, no hands, sideways, one leg, legs spread. Will had been throwing money at me and there was a pile of twenties and fifties at the foot of the pole. I was going to make sure he got his money's worth, even if the money he was throwing was both of ours.

I decided to try a trick I had seen in a few YouTube videos when I was searching for ideas for the choreography. So I climbed to the top of the pole and flipped upside down and placed my feet flat against the ceiling. Then I started walking around the ceiling.

I don't know what happened in that next second, but in the second after that I found myself waking up, flat on my back on the floor with Will hovering over me like Smokey on Friday with a look of shock and terror on his face.

"Baby! Baby! Baby, are you okay? Can you see me?" he asked.

"Yeah, yeah," I moaned. "I can see and hear you."

"Goddamnit, baby! You scared the shit out of me!"

"I'm okay. I'm okay," I said as I started getting up.

"You sure? Don't move too fast," he said as he helped me to my feet.

"Yeah, I'm fine. Jus my pride is hurt. That's all."

"It should be a whole lot more than your pride hurting right about now," he chuckled.

"That shit ain't funny," I said, and then started laughing with him.

"You hit the floor hard as hell, baby. I know the people below us heard that shit if they're at home."

"Whatever!" I slapped his arm. "You hungry? I cooked plenty of food."

"So you're changing the subject now?"

"No, all that twerking has me starving," I said as I dipped a shrimp in cocktail sauce and bit into it.

*   ~   *   ~   *

And so we began our life together. We brought in the new year together in our apartment as happy and content and as in love as any two fools anyone had ever seen. I began cooking even more regularly. Will's clientele had more than doubled, so he definitely needed the help.

Things became even more hectic at tax time because everybody had money and they wanted to spend it all. The demand was definitely there, so we had no choice but to accommodate it by providing the supply. There were times Will would have to deliver the products as soon as they were finished while I was still cooking other batches. He had gained clients in Memphis and small towns in Fayette County, Tennessee as well.

Will left town on a Tuesday going to Memphis to deliver a very large order for two major drug dealers: Big Bang and his brother, Goose. Whoever said 'one monkey don't stop no show' couldn't have been more accurate if they had quoted The Bible. It didn't matter that everyone thought it was just Will cooking that shit. It didn't even matter that it was just the two of us. They had to have it and it had to be as soon as possible. So while Will was gone, I had to start delivering the finished product.

"How are you doing, Beautiful?" one guy asked me. "You Will's girl?"

"Yep," I nodded.

"You got a name?"

"You don't need my name. I just came to handle business. Nothing more, nothing less."

"Alright," he smirked, amused by my feistiness.

"And can we speed this up a little bit? I've got other clients waiting."

"Oh, they can hold on a few minutes, can't they?"

"I suggest you pick up the pace because just like you want your shit, they want theirs too, and in a timely fashion. I don't make my money wait," I told him.

"Alright, alright, little lady," he said as he finished packing money into a grocery bag with a lit cigarette hanging from his lip. "Don't I know you from somewhere, though? You look familiar." He glanced at me out of the corner of his eye.

"I doubt it," I said as I took the bag from him. "Give Will a call when you're ready to conduct your next transaction."

* ~ * ~ *

I didn't know it then, but the guy actually did recognize me, though at that moment he couldn't recall where he had met me. That same buyer made a trip to Memphis to deliver weed to Tristian. Tristian was taking a semester off from school for a broken leg he acquired during an intense rugby game. The broken leg turned out to be a hairline fracture, but he didn't find out until after the school's deadline, so he decided he'd return to his beloved Ivy League in the fall.

"My guy!" Tristian greeted Jason as he opened the door. His parents were at work, as usual, and Tristian was home alone. Even his younger brother had better shit to do than sit around the house all day.

"What it do?" Jason shook Tristian's hand and walked into the house.

"You got a minute? I'll smoke one with you if you can chill for a second. It's a hell of a drive back to Georgia."

"Yeah, that's cool. I got a minute," Jason said as he handed Tristian his package and then followed him upstairs to his bedroom.

"Have a seat," Tristian showed Jason to the chair at his

desk and then sat down opposite him and began breaking down a cigar.

"Nice room you got here," Jason complimented him.

"Thanks. It's my parents' house, you know? I plan to have one twice this size one day with a wife twice as beautiful as my mom."

"Damn, man. You just gone insult your mom?"

"I mean, she's my mom and all, but she ain't a looker, and she's a real bitch. She nags all the time, complains, gets on my damn nerves."

"Damn," Jason shook his head. "I'd never talk about my mom like that. You only get one mom, man. You'd better appreciate her while you got her because when she's gone, ain't no coming back."

"I'm waiting on that day," Tristian told him.

"Who's the chick in the pic? I've seen it in your car too. She's beautiful," Jason asked as he pointed to a picture in a silver frame on the desk.

"That's my best friend and the woman I had hoped to marry," he said as he picked up the frame and stared into my eyes in the picture. "Her name is Bre'ana."

"Oh, I'm sorry," Jason apologized as he took a drag from the blunt.

"For what?" Tristian frowned.

"You said you had hoped to marry her, as in once did but no longer do. People usually use that sense of past tense when the person is deceased." Tristian stared at Jason for a second, taken aback, realizing that he had greatly misjudged him. "Is she not deceased?"

"Umm, no, no," he said. "She's very much alive. It just seems that suddenly any chance I once thought I had of making her my bride was snatched from beneath me by someone who is less than deserving, to say the least."

"'Less than deserving'? How so?" Jason asked. Tristian was almost completely speechless, unable to believe that he was having an intelligent conversation with a guy he had just a few minutes before believed was just as incapable of spelling a word comprised of more than four letters as the person they were discussing.

"He's… ummm… ill-equipped financially. He's irresponsible. He's uneducated. And he's hideous to look at," he explained.

"How do you know all of this to be true?"

"I've studied him, researched him, delved into his background. He's nothing more than a common thug."

"But if this were true, and she prefers him over you- a guy who seems so much more qualified- then why do you still desire her? She's obviously not the woman you believed her to be, nor does she possess the standards you believed her to have. Should that not turn you away from her?" Jason questioned.

"One would think that it would, but somehow that is not the case. I love her. I've loved her for years. Love like the kind of love I have for her does not die easily," Tristian said as he dumped the ashes on the blunt and took another drag.

"Honestly, it sounds to me like you don't love her at all, and I say that for two reasons. One: if you love her, you want her to be happy. Period. This guy makes her happy and yet, you're unsatisfied with that. If you love her, that happiness you see in her eyes would be all that mattered, even if she is happy with someone other than you. Two: the way you've studied him and seek and desire her relentlessly are indications that you are not in love. You're infatuated. It's become a challenge for you, something you have to win. This woman is not some a prize to be won. She is free to make her own decisions to do what she believes is in her best interest. You should reevaluate your feelings." Jason rose to leave. "I'm gonna get out of here, man. I have other stops to make while I'm up here. You just think about what I said."

"Why are you so ready to go all of a sudden? What's up? We haven't even finished the blunt yet."

"Nothing, man. Your girl, man. I just need to get up out of here. That's all." But Tristian noticed Jason's eyes darting at the picture repeatedly as if he had just had a revelation.

"No, man. What about her? You know something I don't?"

"I know her. I mean, I've seen her around the way. That's

all. It ain't shit."

"It must be something because you're suddenly so uncomfortable that you're ready to leave. Tell me what's going on."

"She's…ummm. She's straight, man. I recognize her now. Her man, he's not the common thug you think he is and he's more than capable of taking care of her. Shit, she's been taking care of herself. They've gone into business together."

"Business? What the fuck does he do for a living?"

"Man, dude has to be the biggest drug chef in the South. That man whips up some shit that nobody out here can replicate. Word on the street is that his girl has been instrumental in that. She goes to school for the shit. Most people have never seen her, but I go to some of the same parties they go to, hang with some of the same people. That's how I know her." Niggas talk more than bitches, man. He spilled all of my business like he was getting paid. Niggas on First 48 don't even give it up that fast. They at least get a Coke and a cigarette from the detectives before they narrate the whole story like a book.

"Who told you that? Who told you Bre do that shit?" Tristian yelled, getting in his face.

"Man, chill. It's a whisper in the industry. There's no name to give. But your girl is doing the same thing. Believe that. Look, man. I gotta roll. I got a schedule to keep."

Tristian stared at the picture as he listened to the front door open and close as Jason left and then kissed the glass over my lips.

*   ～   *   ～   *

Will and I were chilling at opposite ends of the bar at the club one night, enjoying the view while tossing back drinks. It was another one of Will's cousin's parties. Neither of us felt like being there, but Will had already promised he'd show up and the made me promise I'd tag along, so we were both stuck.

Guys were approaching me every once in a while, asking me to dance offering to buy me drinks. Will had always taught me to never accept a drink from anyone because nothing in this world is free and every gift came with an expectation. Between the guys trying to holler at me, I was noticing the side eyes and wandering fingers of the bitches who were bold enough to approach Will where he was sitting at the bar.

One particular female kept coming back to the bar to sit next to Will. He'd shoo her off, and thirty or forty-five minutes later, she'd be right back at his right elbow, grinning and touching his arm. Will saw how I was looking at her and chuckled and shook his head, telling me not to start any trouble. I didn't give a fuck. The bitch needed to learn to accept a no.

She walked off again after Will shook his head at her for what must have been the fifth time. I tossed the last of my Hurricane back and sucked on the orange slice that had been perched on the rim of the glass. Will squinted his eyes at me, catching the enticement. I ran my tongue around the outside of the peel and then sucked the middle to pull the inside off of the rim. You could've thumped Will and he would've fallen over. The look on his face was priceless.

I saw Suzie the Stalker trying to make her way through the crowded dance floor back to Will, so I got up and went down the bar to occupy the vacant seat next to my man. Of course, Suzie didn't like that.

"Excuse me," she frowned as she approached. "I was sitting there."

"Well, thank you for keeping my seat warm," I said with a smile.

"No, I don't think you understand," she said as she stepped into my personal space. "That's my seat. You need to get up."

"I don't think you understand. It's my seat now and you need to walk away."

"Walk away? Bitch, you'd better get up before you get carried away," she threatened.

"And just who exactly is going to do that?" I laughed at her.

"Oh, so it's funny, huh?" she said as she stepped even closer. "We'll see who's laughing when I slap your ass out of my damn seat."

"Bitch, you ain't gone slap no damn body! Now go on about your business because I promise you this is not what you want," I assured her.

"I'm not going any damn where. I've been sitting over here enjoying my evening with my new boo and we were just about to get out of here and go get something to eat, so I suggest you step aside."

Up until this point, Will had been facing forward, trying to ignore the situation, and shaking his head at how unreal the predicament was. When the young lady called him her new boo and advised me that they were just about to leave together (which I knew was so far from the truth you needed binoculars to find it), he turned to interject, but I didn't even let him get one word in.

"Bitch, let me tell you something. Not only are you lying, but you're delusional as well. You see, this here is MY man. From the top of his head to the bottom of his feet. The bed he sleeps in and every piece of food he eats. That's all me, sweetheart."

"Oh, it is, huh? So you're just going to sit here and let her talk to me like this after we've been having fun all night?" she asked Will. Will opened his mouth to speak, but I cut him off again.

"Having fun? Girl, please! He's been trying to get rid of you all night! Ha!"

"So it's funny, bitch?" she said, her face turning red in embarrassment. "Bitch, I'll slap the smirk right off of your face."

"See, I've been trying to be cool, but what you're not

going to do is stand here and keep threatening me. Either you get your ass away from me and my man, or I'm going to have to remove you myself," I gave it to her straight.

She opened her mouth to say something that was going to start with the word "bitch," but by the time she got the B out of her mouth I had punched her in her teeth and was on top of her on the floor pounding her face.

"Bre! Bre! Bre, stop!" I heard Will's voice in the distance. I must've zoned out, but when I snapped back the chick was on the floor with blood pouring from her nose, both eyes blacked, and knots all over her face and forehead. "Come on, Bre. Let's go," Will said as he tugged at my arm, but I didn't move. I just stood there looking down at the unconscious bleeding woman. "Bre, let's go! We gotta go!"

"Bacardi Barbie, bitch! Ask about me," I said as I stepped over her. I followed Will out to the parking lot and hopped into the passenger seat of his black Challenger.

"Can't take your ass nowhere," he said as he glanced at me and started laughing as he drove. I just shrugged my shoulders nonchalantly and then began examining my nails for damage.

Chapter 14

Will and I got behind on orders, so I spent my Spring Break catching up on the large batches of meth and heroin he hadn't been able to produce. We were working so hard and manufacturing so much product that Will couldn't deliver it all, so I began making deliveries too.

At first, Will was completely against it. I was still supposed to be completely behind the scenes. Eventually, he realized that just wasn't a possibility anymore. Either I was going to have to help with the deliveries too, we were going to have to bring in a third person to pick up our slack, or we were going to have to turn away money. We had a method with our duo, so of course, neither of us wanted to bring in a third person to disrupt our flow and cut into our profits, and turning away money was just not an option.

I developed a new routine for my deliveries. Will started me out with a small number of clients. There were no phone calls needed at all. They knew when I was coming. I knew where to go. It all worked like clockwork. Will had taken me to buy a gun, so I carried my cute little pink Smith & Wesson .38 in my handbag everywhere I went, and I always remained aware of my surroundings. It seemed with every change necessary, Will and I adapted with little or no difficulty and continued with daily life without so much as an argument or even a breakdown in communication. There were no hiccups.

Will had started loading my deliveries into my truck for me while I was in class during the week. He'd drive out to the house and pick everything up and come up to the school, park next to my truck that I always parked in a back corner of the parking lot, load my deliveries, and then take off to drop his own.

One Tuesday, I was out making my normal runs. I had been feeling sick all day, so I was uneasy with all of the drops. I pulled up to the last house for the day at my normal time: nine-thirty that evening. It was always dark, but it always went smoothly. This time was no exception. I made the delivery to Jean-Michael, a dread-headed Rasta who loved watching Love Boat and Gilligan's Island. But on my way back to my truck, a hand suddenly reached out and grabbed me. Before I could even scream another hand covered my mouth and nose with a handkerchief that was doused in some sort of liquid.

When I woke up it was daylight again and I had no clue where I was or what had happened. I had a horrible headache that the sunlight was aggravating and my body was sore from lying on the flat wooden floor. My ankles and wrists were bound with duct tape and there was another strip covering my mouth.

Sitting up on the floor, trying my best not to panic, I surveyed my surroundings. I was in the kitchen of a house I had never visited. It was obvious that no one else had been visiting the house either. The dust was thick enough to write my name in and the decorations were very dated. The house was silent. The refrigerator wasn't running. No heating or air conditioning unit was clicking on and off.

"The electricity must not be on," I said to myself aloud, my heart racing.

Will had prepared me for a lot of scenarios. We had walked through the procedure for being robbed for the money or jacked for the goods. I knew how to appropriately (and inappropriately) react to women approaching me about Will when he wasn't present. I knew how to refuse to bargain or negotiate on prices when conducting transactions, and I knew how to avoid all attention from all forms of law enforcement. But never did Will and I ever think that anyone would be bold enough to actually kidnap me. I had no idea what to do in this situation, even though I was trained to survive in most general predicaments.

I couldn't tell how long I had been unconscious. Judging by the interior of the house, I could tell that whoever had abducted me would return. Though the house was old and dusty, it was well maintained. There were no leaks in the ceilings or rotting floorboards. The house actually meant something to someone. There was a reason it was being kept and kept up.

I knew I wouldn't be able to keep my balance if I attempted to stand and walk and if I fell over I wouldn't be able to put my hands out to catch my fall, so I scooted across the floor to look into the doorway that led to the next room. It was a living room full of very out-dated furniture. There were light spots in the paint on the walls where framed photographs once hung but had been taken down, empty spaces on the mantle, gaping holes on the end tables.

"So this is probably somebody I know. They don't want me to see the family photos," I thought to myself. "That's okay though. Whoever it is, they'll be back. They didn't kill me when they had the chance, which is their mistake. They obviously want me or need me for something. More than likely, they're trying to get close to Will. They always use the women as the weak little pawn. The problem is that I'm not weak, I plopped myself onto the sofa and stretched out, and neither am I a pawn. Of course, Will will come looking for me, but be careful of the wrath you call upon yourself. With that, I laid down, made myself comfortable, and awaited my captor's return.

* ~ * ~ *

By that point, Will already knew something had to have been wrong. My phone was going straight to voicemail and he hadn't heard from me since the day before. He hadn't been able to sleep when I didn't come home that night, so he had been out combing the streets for any sign of me or my truck. When he turned up empty-handed, he started making phone calls. By the time I stretched out on that old dusty sofa, Will, his entire posse, and seven of his cousins were in the Atlanta streets actively searching for me

Five days went by. Will had put the word out on the street for every dope boy on every corner of every block to keep their ears to the ground and eyes open for any sign of me. But on the sixth day, he called my parents.

My mother, of course, was not too thrilled to hear from the man her daughter had abandoned her for. When Will explained to her the reason for his call, her first assumption was that Will and I had gotten into some sort of argument and I had left him. But when he explained that we had been living together and not only had I not been home in nearly a week, but there were no signs that I had taken anything with me, she realized that this was no lover's spat. I was truly missing.

My parents came down to Atlanta from Memphis to do their own investigation. They walked through the entire apartment looking for any sign of a struggle, any possible clue, or anything at all that maybe Will had missed. Nothing.

"Mr. Braxton, I don't know what to do. I'm not into it with anyone and neither is she. I have no clue who could have taken her or even where she was taken," Will said with his head in his hands as he sat on our sofa.

"We've got to call the police and file a report," my mother said in tears.

"No! We can't! We can't get the police involved," Will protested.

"But we have to!" my mother insisted.

"No, we can't. No police," Will rose to his feet.

"Young man, exactly why can't we go to the police?" my father asked sternly as he approached Will.

"I…I can't exactly say, but just trust me. We can't get the police involved. I'm going to do everything I can to find her and bring her back home as soon and as safely as possible, but, please, just let me handle this," Will begged my parents.

"You're goddamned right you're going to do everything

you can!" my mother spat at him. "This is all your fault! I don't know what's going on here, but I know this mess that my baby is caught up in has something to do with you, and you better believe you're going to find my little girl or die trying because if you don't, I'm going to kill you in a way so slow and painful you're going to wish they had taken you instead."

"Brenda, that's enough!" my father said as he pulled her out of Will's face. "You have no right to accuse this young man of anything, let alone threaten him. Look at him. Can't you see he's hurting enough already? Whether our daughter's disappearance has something to do with him or not, had he not called us, we would not even know Bre'ana was missing."

"So what do you want me to do? Thank him? Ha! He'd better be glad you're not prying my fingers from around his neck right now."

"I'm sure your presence is choking him enough, Brenda," my father said before he could catch himself.

"Really, Gerald? Whose side are you on here?" she fumed.

"It's not about sides, Brenda. Our daughter is missing. I'm on Bre'ana's side. I care nothing about how you feel about her boyfriend. That is completely irrelevant. Right now, my concern is locating my daughter and bringing her home in one piece!"

"I can't believe you're going to stand here and disregard the fact that this entire situation is a direct result of her being involved with this hoodlum! Bre'ana is a good kid. She makes wise, sound decisions. She's smart and highly intelligent. You know just like I do that she would have never gotten herself into this situation on her own. And you stand here and act like all of that is irrelevant," she yelled at my father as Will stood there watching them fall apart. "And you have the nerve to even entertain whether or not we can trust the fate of our only child being left in the hands of the likes of him," she said with a look of utter disgust on her face.

"You say that as though you're questioning my judgment," my father challenged her.

"So what? Maybe I am," she said, looking him squarely in the eyes.

"Let me explain something to you, Brenda. You may have made so much money and locked up so many criminals that you've forgotten what life is like for the average American, but I have not. You can have all of the higher learning, the degrees, the commendations, the cases under your belt, but one thing you have no clue about is what it's like to be a black man in America, especially in the South. I do. I know what it's like. I live it every single day. Your heart may be so hardened that your eyes have become blinded to love, but mine has not. Look at that young man, Brenda! Look at him!" my father yelled as he pointed at Will. "Look into his eyes. Don't you see his pain hidden deep within? This is the person our daughter spends all of her time with. This is the man who eats her cooking, who rubs her feet, who sleeps with our daughter wrapped in his arms every single night. He loves her. Don't you see it? Imagine how lonely he must feel without her here. This entire ordeal has been a nightmare for him and has interrupted his whole life. I don't care how you feel about him. This is his home. He is the man of this house, and I can guarantee you the only reason he hasn't cursed you out and put you the fuck out of his house is because you're Bre'ana's mother and he's hoping one day you'll be his mother-in-law. So while he stands here and bites his tongue out of respect, I'm going to stand up for him. You may not like it, but you have no choice but to put your trust in him because that's exactly what I'm going to do. Obviously there are some extenuating circumstances surrounding Bre'ana's disappearance if William doesn't want us to call the police, so we're going to let him handle this, and if I hear anything that doesn't fall in line with that from you, there will be a whole new set of consequences you've never seen before."

My mother was speechless. My father had never talked to her like that. She was accustomed to always getting her way with my father because he never really spoke up about anything. This time was much different.

"Do I make myself clear, Brenda?" he asked. My mother simply nodded in response. "Good. Let's go."

My mother grabbed her cardigan and purse and headed to the door as my father approached Will.

"Son, I sure hope you know what you're doing. My daughter's life is in your hands," he said to him. "I'm sorry you had to hear all of that. I'll take care of Bre'ana's mother. You just concentrate on finding Bre'ana and don't take too long. The second you waste could be the second you're too late getting to her. I'm putting my faith in you."

"Yes, sir," Will nodded as he offered his hand to my father.

"I won't let you down."

My father shook Will's hand and looked him square in the eyes and said, "I know you won't, son, and for what it's worth, I'm so sorry. I can only imagine what you're feeling right now. Just remember that Bre'ana is my daughter and my only child. I love her just as much as you do in a completely different way. That doesn't mean I love her anymore or you love her any less. I just want you to know that I understand how you feel. If you need anything to help you find her, you let me know, even if you need me to come help you myself. Whatever it is, I'm here one hundred percent."

"Yes, sir. Thank you, sir. Thank you," Will said as he hugged my father. Of all of the things that were said, it was what was left unsaid that spoke the loudest, that sent Will on a mission to search relentlessly for me.

Chapter 15

During that first week, I was visited every day at noon by a crackhead who came bearing cheap five dollar boxes from fast food restaurants. He was an older white guy with long, scraggly blonde hair, track marks in his arms, and a tattoo of a rebel flag on his neck. I had never seen him before, but he seemed to be well aware of who I was.

The first day he came, he brought fried chicken and threatened to slit my throat if I screamed when he took the tape off my mouth. I ate the leg, thigh, mashed potatoes, and biscuit in silence and paid him no attention at all. When I finished eating, he taped my hands and mouth back up and helped me back onto the sofa. When he left, he locked the door after checking all of the windows and doors, and I was left alone.

This went on for three days. On the fourth day, when he left, I got curious, so I scooted my way through the house, exploring in the dark. I knocked over two lamps and stubbed my toe twice, but I didn't care. I was looking for any clue to why I had been kidnapped and by whom because it was obvious that the guy who was visiting me every day had no real business to conduct with me.

When he returned the next day and saw the pieces of the broken lamps scattered across the floor, he became furious. After cleaning up the fragments, he got on the phone and told someone what I had done. When he hung up, he left for about forty-five minutes, which I spent talking shit in my head. He came back in dragging a heavy chain with large locks attached to both ends. I tried my best to scream as loud as I could, terrified of what I knew he was about to do, but the screams were too muffled by the tape to even escape the walls of the house.

"Shut up, bitch, and quit squirming," were the first words he ever said to me. He actually believed that I was going to allow him to chain my ass to anything inside of that house. I kicked and tossed as hard as I could, but deep down I knew I couldn't avoid it. He snatched me up by the collar and looked into my eyes.

"I'm going to have to chain you up since you don't know how to sit your ass still," he told me, the stench of cheap cigarettes and ever cheaper beer on his breath. "Now be still and this won't hurt."

I didn't know who the fuck he thought I was, but I had been cooperative long enough. My arms were already tired and sore from being taped behind me. My inner ankle on both feet was sore from being pressed against each other. If he thought I was just going to sit there and allow him to add a chain to my misery, he had another thing coming.

I shook my head profusely as he tried to wrap the chain around me and then squirmed so much that he kept dropping the chain. When he dropped one end at an angle that caused him to have to bend down next to me, I kicked him square in the face. He jumped up screaming and holding his eye.

"Stupid bitch!" he yelled and then back-handed me so

hard it echoed in my ears. I forced myself to suck up the tears that formed in my eyes. I wasn't going to let him get to me, let alone break me. This shit was bigger than him and I knew it. He wasn't calling the shots. He was a flunky, a send out. He was nothing, and I knew I should anticipate more, worse, harsher.

So I kicked him again, this time in the stomach. He yelled out in pain, grabbed my throat, and squeezed so hard that I didn't have to wonder if his fingers had left prints on my neck. While I struggled to catch my breath when he let go, he wrapped the chain around me tightly and the lock clicked closed. Then he snatched the other end and pulled it tight as he wrapped it around the old radiator heater by the wall. I knew I was stuck. There was no getting out of that shit without the key. I was fucked.

When he had double-checked that the chain was secure, he removed the tape from my ankles and wrists. I forced my face to remain unmoved and emotionless.

He turned to walk away and then said over his shoulder, "You can take that strip off your mouth yourself. I suppose you're going to take it off anyway. But just know that if you scream no one will hear you. You're out in the middle of nowhere. You might as well save your breath." Then he left. Without feeding me. And I was there alone for three days.

*　～　*　～　*

While I was chained to the damn heater like I was Christina Ricci, Will was in the streets searching high and low for any sign of me or anyone who knew where I might be. In between, he was still trying to keep up with the orders. He had slowed down production without me there to help him, of course, but he still was trying to keep our clientele. He was finding it difficult to focus while he was cooking, having become so accustomed to having me in the kitchen with him to keep him company and help him with the orders.

I'd lay there in that living room all day thinking of Will. I missed everything about him, so I could only imagine how he was feeling. I wondered where he was and what he was doing. The not knowing was killing me. My mind wandered off sometimes and I even wondered if Will had called Toya out of physical desperation. I cried at night while thinking of that possibility, praying that he hadn't betrayed me again, hoping that he loved me enough to only desire me.

In reality, Will hadn't even looked at another woman and he certainly hadn't called his ex. Sex was the furthest thing from his mind at that time. He was heartbroken and searching desperately for me.

As time went by, he became more and more worried and felt like even more of a failure with each passing day. He had done everything he could think of doing and asked everyone he could think of asking within those first two weeks.

He came home one night after finishing his runs and looked at the sheets on the bed and couldn't take it. A pair of my earrings and the chain he had bought me were laying on my nightstand. One of my jackets was hanging from the bed-post on my side of the bed. He walked over to the jacket and buried his face in the fleece to inhale my scent. That's when the tears finally came.

He hadn't given himself time to be sad or hurt. He had jumped into go-mode to find me, but his failure had made the situation finally sink in with him. The tears flowed freely as he sat on the edge of the bed holding my jacket, but they also made him angry. Will knew me and how sweet and innocent my heart was. He knew I'd never leave him that way, and the fact that someone had taken me away from him enraged him. Everything in our apartment reminded him of me, made him miss me even more, and made him that much angrier.

* ~ * ~ *

I was asleep on the couch one morning with the chain pulled as far as it could go when the front door opened. I hadn't been able to sleep well due to my growling stomach and the hunger pains, so it took nothing to wake me up. I frowned at the sunlight as it poured in through the door.

"Wake the fuck up," a familiar voice said. It wasn't the same crackhead that had been tending to me, but my eyes were so swollen and puffy from crying all night that I couldn't make out the figure in the doorway. I barely moved as he approached, and when he made it to me, he snatched me up and slapped me. "I said wake up!" he yelled. I instantly recognized the voice.

"Tristian?" I mumbled.

"Yeah, it's me," he said. "In the flesh. Are you hungry?"

"I haven't eaten in four days," I told him.

"I've got some hash browns from Waffle House here," he

said as he showed me the bag with the plate inside, "for the woman who's ready to be mine."

I looked at him like he was crazy.

"Are you serious? You march in here after you've had me hostage for a week in the care of a crackhead who slapped and choked me. You slap me and then think I'm going to volunteer to date you for some Waffle House? I don't give a fuck how hungry I am," I said as I plopped back down on the couch. "Bitch, I'll die of starvation before I even consider being with you."

"Oh, you're going to be mine or your ass will never leave this damn house," he assured me.

"Bitch, please! You got me fucked up. You honestly think my man isn't going to come looking for me?"

"Oh, he's already looking for you. He's been looking for you since the first night you didn't come home. I give it to him. Your boy had quite a bit of pull in the streets. The problem is that we're not in Kansas anymore, Toto," he laughed. "He wouldn't know where to even begin looking for you and you're so far away from civilization that no one will ever find you."

"Where the fuck am I, Tristian? Is this your folks' house?"

"It used to be my grandparents' house before they passed. My father keeps it just because he grew up here. Nobody ever comes out here. Ever. And the nearest neighbor is a mile away," he revealed. Just from that information alone, I knew

I was nowhere near Atlanta. I remembered Tristian's father mentioning that he grew up in Fayette County in Tennessee. Tristian had somehow had me kidnapped in Atlanta and driven all the way to the county next to Memphis.

"Tristian, what's the point of this? Really. What the fuck is going on with you? Is this really the kind of relationship you want? Do you want to intimidate me into being with you? That's not love, Tristian, and even if I agreed to be with you, that shit wouldn't even last. I'm already with someone. I'm in a relationship. I'm in love," I told him.

"Stop saying that! Don't say that! You are not in love with that nothing! What is it? Is it because you fucked him? Is that what it takes? Some dick? Cause I can give you that," he said as he started unbuckling his pants.

"Tristian, that has nothing to do with it," I said as I rolled my eyes at him.

"That's exactly what it is," he said as his pants fell to the floor. "You want some dick? I'll give you some dick."

"Tristian, if you don't get the fuck away from me." He was getting on my nerves with his ignorance.

"Come on, baby. Pull these down," he said as he tugged at the leggings I had now been wearing for over a week.

"Tristian, stop! I am not about to fuck you. I don't want anything to do with you!"

"Oh, you're going to fuck me today. You're going to take

all of this dick today," he said as he dropped his boxers. I had known Tristian all of my life. I had never seen this side of him, and I had never seen his dick before. He should've kept that shit that way because I was disappointed with both.

"No, I'm not. Now get away from me," I told him.

"Get away from you? You let that nothing ass nigga pop up and fuck you, but I've been knowing you since we were kids and you tell me to get away from you? Naw, you gone give me some pussy today!"

He pulled at my leggings again and I pushed him away from me. He came right back trying to take my leggings off and I pushed him even harder. The back of his hand made contact with my cheek and sounded off, and at that point, I lost all consideration for who I was fighting. This mother fucker had slapped me twice in one day. He had me fucked up.

I punched Tristian in his left eye and followed it with a string of punches when I saw the initial punch had stunned him. If he wanted to fight, I was ready to square up. He may have known me most of our lives, but he didn't know my hands were decent and anybody could get it.

When he tried to fight me back, I swung harder, and he resorted to trying to grab my hands. When he finally caught my left hand, I kneed him in the nuts and shoved him back as he let out a high pitched wail. He fell onto the coffee table which immediately broke under his weight. I stood over him with my fists still balled, making sure he was down.

"Ahhh! You bitch!" he yelled. He pulled his boxers and his pants up from around his ankles and limped to the door. "Your ass gone starve for that shit, bitch!" he said before slamming the door. I looked at the Waffle House bag on the other side of the room and back at the door as Tristian's car crunk up and pulled off. It was going to take some work, but starving was what I was not going to do as long as there was food in that house.

Chapter 16

Will got out of the black Challenger and closed the door. He stared at the black rims, remembering how I had reacted the day he had come home with the car. I loved the black rims on the black car. They made it look so sophisticated. I was smiling like a Cheshire cat when I saw it and instantly fell in love. Will was jealous. He had hardly ever let me drive it or ride in it because he said I loved that car more than I loved him. He was joking, of course, but the memory at that moment stabbed him deep in his heart.

He walked up to the front door of the small, green house in the neighborhood that was once quiet with the exception of children's laughter but had turned into a haven for gang activity and drug transactions. He reached up to knock, but the door was opened before his knuckles could make contact with the glass of the security door.

"My guy!" the heavy-set man smiled widely as he unlocked the door.

"What's up, Bang?" Will greeted him with an unenthusiastic handshake and a hug.

"What's up witcha, my nigga?" Big Bang smiled as Will sat down on the living room sofa.

"Man…shit. Nothing at all," Will shook his head.

"You got my shit?" he inquired.

"Yeah. It's all there," Will said as he tossed a duffel bag to Big Bang.

"That's what's up," he said as he handed Will another bag. Will sat the bag at his feet and sat back on the sofa.

"You ain't gone count your shit?" Big Bang frowned.

"Naw, I trust you, man," Will said. Big Bang looked at him for a few seconds, reading him, and then shrugged it off.

"That's what's up. Look, Lil Will, man. I've been meaning to mention to you that my customers have been saying the quality is a little off lately. It ain't quite the same. You know, I don't do the shit, so I never know, but that's what they're coming back telling me."

"Yeah, man, I know. I'm used to having my girl helping me. She was the one who developed the recipe we were using. I cook it up pretty well myself, but my mind just ain't right. My heart ain't in it," Will confessed.

"Well, where is she? What's going on?" Big Bang asked as his brother Goose came from the back bedroom and greeted Will.

"Where is who? What's up, Lil Will?"

"Somebody kidnapped my girl, man. I think. She's been missing for a few weeks now. I've searched high and low, everywhere I could think of, and I can't find her."

"Had y'all been arguing? You think she ran off?" Big Bang asked him.

"Hell naw. Everything was copasetic. We get along just fine. We don't fight and argue and shit. Every day is full of fun and laughter, some crazy ass prank she's pulling, or some goofy performance. We're always having fun. There wasn't a reason for her to run off."

"So this isn't just your girl. This is your wife. She's the one," Goose said.

"Hell yeah, man. That's my baby. She's my world, man. That girl has my whole heart."

"So what are you doing about it, nigga?" Goose frowned.

"I don't know what else to do or where to look," he shook his head.

"Man, you've got a whole crew," Big Bang frowned. "You didn't put your niggas to work?"

"Man, I put the whole team to work on this shit, Bang. My crew and my cousins. I had everybody out here looking for her."

"And you still turned up empty-handed," Goose shook his head.

"I don't know what to do anymore. I can't sleep. I'm never hungry. I have to make myself eat. I just get in the car and drive. I never know where I'm going. I just go. I go home when I miss her, and it makes me miss her even more. So I leave. It's just a big cycle of pointless coming and going. Somebody got me out here looking stupid, and I promise the shit ain't gone be pretty when I catch them," Will vowed.

"The last time you were telling me about your girl, didn't you say she was from here?" Goose asked. "Did you check with her folks?"

"Yeah, and they even came down to Atlanta when I called, but they don't know where she is either. They're doing me the favor of not calling the police while I try to handle this shit myself."

"Damn, man. Well, we'll definitely keep our ears open for you. You need to get your crew on that shit, though. Y'all start beating mother fuckers' asses, somebody gone tell it."

"I got you," Will said as he stood up to leave. "Y'all just let me know if you hear anything." He shook their hands and left out the door. Standing at the front of the car, his hands in his pockets, duffel bag thrown over his shoulder, he shook his head at the car as the memory cut deep into the wound yet again.

*　～　*　～　*

Four more days went by before Tristian came back. I had used a leg from the broken table to pull the Waffle House bag over to me. Tristian had said it had hashbrowns, but there was also cheese eggs, two pieces of sausage, three slices of bacon, and two waffles inside as well. I ate half of the plate that first night and then hid the rest under the couch. I didn't eat the

177

next day, as I was expecting Tristian to return. On the third night, I ate the rest of the food and prayed it would last me until I got my hands on some more.

Tristian came stumbling in two nights later, carrying a bottle of Bacardi in one hand and an almost empty bottle of Burnett's in the other. I shook my head at him in disgust. He was beyond drunk. He could barely walk, so I was wondering how he had driven to the house.

"You fucking bitch," he said in a low slur. "I leave you out here all this time and you're still alive, huh?" He tripped over his own feet and almost fell, causing me to laugh. "So it's funny? The shit is funny? You think it's funny? We'll see how much you laugh with my dick down your throat… ole funky bitch!"

"I ain't gone be too many more bitches, Tristian. This little situation has really brought out your true colors. You're hella disrespectful," I said calmly.

"Yeah, and you're a helluva ho, stupid bitch! I've heard all about you, you slut. They say you get a couple of drinks in you and turn the fuck up. You turn into a real freak junt, dancing on counters and tables, twerking all over the place, ass just shaking and bouncing everywhere," he shouted. Twisting the cap off the bottle of Bacardi, he thrust it in my direction. "Here," he said. "Drink up. Let's see what this little performance you do looks like."

I just sat there looking at him. I didn't even attempt to move. Tristian had lost his damn mind. For all he knew, I hadn't eaten in four days, and he expected me to toss back a bottle of liquor on an empty stomach. Even I knew better than that.

"Why are you just sitting there," he snarled. "I said drink up."

"I'm straight on that shit," I declined.

"No, you're not," he said as he snatched me up from the sofa. "I said drink and that's exactly what the fuck you're going to do. You think I won't beat your ass? Huh? You think I won't kill you? Bitch, I'll snap your fucking neck," he said with his lips an inch away from my face.

"If you were going to kill me, you would have done it by now, Tristian. I suggest you get your drunk ass out of my face," I said calmly.

"You're right. I don't want to kill you. I wanted you to be my wife. I wanted to marry you and have three kids together and a dog and live happily ever after. You're making this shit harder than it has to be. Instead of marrying me and being treated right and spoiled, you're gallivanting around with that hoodlum and damaging both your image and your body," he admitted.

"Damaging my body how?" I frowned.

"You're drunk every weekend and sometimes in the middle of the week too. And you've completely lost your mind for the BBC," he said.

"The BBC?" I laughed. "What the fuck do you know

about a BBC, Tristian?"

"Oh please! I watch enough Porn Hub and X Videos! I know what he's doing to you and why you've lost your damn mind over him," he scoffed.

"You're the one who's lost their mind, Tristian. You've gone clean over the deep end. You're obsessed. You're delusional. Look around you! We're in an abandoned house in the middle of nowhere surrounded by trees and woods. You've fucking kidnapped me and you're holding me hostage! And until when? Huh, Tristian? When are you going to let me go? How long is long enough? I've missed two weeks of classes. I have a life to get back to. It's been too long already. When are you going to give this up?"

"Never!" he shouted. "I'm never going to give it up until things are the way they were supposed to be. You were supposed to be mine. I'll never give it up until you finally see the light and tell me you'll be mine until the end of time."

"So you're going to keep me here forever then? Because I don't want you, Tristian. When will you understand and accept that? I don't want you!"

"Yes, you do!" he screamed. "Yes, you do!" He turned the bottle of Bacardi upside down over my head, drenching me in the alcohol. I gasped in shock and the swung at him, landing a blow to his left eye. He screamed out in pain, holding his eye, and then screamed again when the liquor from his wet hands burned his eye. "Ugh! Fuck! Stupid bitch!" He stepped towards me and I readied myself in anticipation of a fight.

"You hit me and I swear I'll lay your ass out," I warned him.

"You just punched me in my eye!" he wailed while moving his hand to reveal a swollen eye that was changing colors with a crimson red eyeball.

"You're goddamned right I did! You just poured a whole bottle of rum on me. I've been wearing these same clothes for two weeks and there's no telling how much longer you're going to have me still wearing this shit. You haven't even been feeding me, but you show up here with alcohol trying to make me drink it. You pulled your dick out and tried to make me fuck you the other day. Hell yeah, I punched you, and I really should light your ass up with more blows than that, trick!"

"Trick?"

"Hell yeah, trick!"

"Bitch, I got your trick," he said and then snatched my head back by my hair. "You think this shit is a game. I'm going to fuck your pretty little brains out and make you beg me to take you as my wife."

"I'll rot to death in this hell hole before that ever happens. That's on every unborn child I haven't had yet," I told him. He immediately slapped me and I felt my cheek begin to swell. He tossed me onto the sofa and then kicked me in my stomach with his boot. I was screaming on the inside, but a part of me just refused to give him the satisfaction.

"Take off these mother fucking leggings," he said as he

181

pulled at my pants again. This shit was getting old with me.

"Tristian, get the fuck away from me."

"Take off these pants, bitch!"

"I'm not having sex with you. Get away from me."

"I said take them off," he growled.

"I'm not taking them off. Now get the fuck away from me before I beat your ass again, you drunk pathetic piece of shit!"

"So that's what it is? You think because I've been drinking you can beat my ass?" he said as he leaned too far over and then misstepped and fell onto the pile of remnants of the coffee table.

"It doesn't have anything to do with you being drunk. You're a piece of shit. You claim you love me, but it's obvious you don't know what love is. You can't possibly expect me to believe that you love me when you're starving me and beating me. You're calling me out of my name and trying to rape me. My parents aren't perfect, but they taught me what love, real love, truly is, and this," I waved my hand at him and the house we were in, "in no way fits into that definition. If you loved me, you'd want me to be happy. You'd want to see me smile. Instead, you're making me cry and making my face swell and bruise. That's not love, Tristian. That's not a love that I want to be a part of. If you love me, let me go."

"No," he said as he shook his head and rose to his feet. He left out of the door, slamming it behind him, and I listened to his car drive away.

I cried out into the night, tired of being held in a cold house with no one to talk to, tired of missing my man, tired of the pains in my stomach from the endless hunger. I was tired of peeing and shitting in a bucket in the corner, feeling like an animal in the wild. It was degrading and embarrassing. I just prayed that someone would find me before I wasted away.

Chapter 17

Will checked our mailbox the next morning and found a letter in the stack of bills. It had been hand-addressed with no return address, and the postmark was from West Memphis, Arkansas. He looked around him to see if anyone was watching, but there was no one outside at all. The kids in the complex were already gone to school. Their parents were already gone to work. He went back inside and closed and locked the door.

Plopping down on the edge of the sofa, Will took a deep breath as his heart began to race. He didn't know why, but he knew there was something inside of that envelope that was going to throw him a hint at my whereabouts.

Opening the plain white envelope that was meant to hold a greeting card, he pulled out a sheet of white paper that had been folded twice. Seeing no blood on it, he felt it was safe. When he unfolded the paper, his eyes grew wide at what he read:

MARRON BITCH

YOU HAVE EVERYTHING

I HAVE NOTHING

PREPARE YOUR SOUL FOR DEATH

KWEEN PEN

THE TIME IS UPON YOU BITCH

He immediately recognized the quote from "The Body-guard;" the letters were cut from magazines and newspapers just like the letter in the movie. He took it as an indication of my kidnapper's intentions, which sent him into an emotional spiral.

Will screamed out in a raspy, low growl that shook the walls. If our neighbors had been home, the police would've been knocking at the door. His emotional anguish was pissing him off. The torture was only motivating him even more. He instantly picked up his phone.

"Cuz...look, get everybody together and meet me at the spot in twenty minutes. Cuz, fuck all that. Get everybody you can and head that way. Yeah. Yeah. Aight. Love cuz."

He looked at the letter again and screamed again, this time picking up two plates off of the kitchen counter and shattering them against the wall.

"Breeeeeeeeeeeeeee!" he screamed out. "Bre'ana, baby, where are you? I'm coming for you, baby. Just come home to me. Just fight until I get there. I'm coming. Wherever you are."

*　～　　*　　～　　*

The spot was Will's old apartment. I had initially asked him to let the apartment go once the lease was up, but Will make a valid point when he argued that he didn't want people coming to our house where we laid our heads to do any kind

185

of business.

"Your place, when it becomes our place, will be a safe haven, a place of peace, a sanctuary. We go home to escape everything we deal with when we're in the streets. We never bring the streets home with us," he had told me and then kissed me gently. "I'm going to keep the old apartment to conduct business. I don't even want many people to know where we live."

"But you had people coming there when you were living there," I argued.

"Yeah, and it was just me there, and you also see what kind of drama that brought," he reminded me. "I have you to protect now, and I'm not going to let anything happen to you unless it happens to me first," he promised. "The best way to keep you protected is to keep your home the safe haven that it has always been for you. I don't want you to change anything on account of me being there. It's perfect just the way it is. Just move your dresses over a little in the closet and clear me out two drawers in the dresser. That's it. The home we share is the home you are most comfortable in. My mother always said that a happy wife makes a happy home."

"Oh, so I'm your wife now?" I raised an eyebrow at him.

"One day, yes, I do intend to make you my wife, my queen. I'd be a fool not to. You've already changed my whole life. You're my world, my whole heart. Yes, baby. You're going to be my wife one day," he told me.

Will opened the door as twelve of his closest friends and

186

family members filed inside. A few of them took seats on the sofa and chair, and the others stood with their arms folded, waiting for Will to speak.

"I know this was very last minute, but I need everybody's help with finding Bre," he told them.

"Lil Will, man, we've looked everywhere already. We done beat two dozen niggas' asses for you. I don't know where the hell baby girl is, but she's nowhere near Atlanta, cuz. We would've found her by now," his oldest cousin, Bernard- Lil Nard for short- told him.

"I got this letter in the mail today," he said as he unfolded the paper and handed it to his youngest cousin, Alexander- A-town for short- who was sitting to his right.

"What the fuck?" A-town said.

"Shit is crazy right? This mother fucker is playing with me, but this shit ain't funny. We gotta find her."

"Yo ,we gone straight murder this nigga when we find him, cuz," Lil Nard said.

"That's not even a question. We gotta find his ass first though. Y'all hit the streets again tough. Comb the city with a fine-tooth comb. We're missing something somewhere. We're overlooking something. She was definitely here when she was taken. Somebody knows something that they're not telling us. You find that person, you get that information, and you beat his ass for not telling us without us having to come looking for them. We run this shit around here. Y'all got that?" Everyone shook their heads and Will let them leave, but Lil Nard and A-town stayed behind.

"Cuz, me and A-town been talking," Lil Nard said when everyone else had left. "We think we're going about this shit the wrong way. It's like you said: we're missing something somewhere- something important."

"Okay, so what do y'all suggest we do differently?"

"You can let everybody else keep doing what they're doing. I'm sure they'll come up with some kind of information," A-town told him. "Me and Nard, though, we know you, cuz. We know what kind of business you run, cuz. We need to retrace Bre'ana's steps. We need to know what her daily routine is, or at least what she was supposed to be doing that day. Where was she supposed to be going? That way we'll know where to start looking. If we don't actually find her, we'll be able to at least get some kind of helpful information."

"Aight," Will nodded. "Y'all sit down." Will went to the kitchen and grabbed a few sheets of paper and a pen and then sat down on the sofa "So business has been booming ever since I let Bre'ana help me cook the drugs. I had to allow Bre'ana to help me deliver the shit too to keep up with the demand," he explained.

"Do you think one of the buyers snatched her?" Lil Nard asked, rubbing his beard.

"I'm not sure, but I don't believe so. You have to remember that Bre'ana is my most valuable asset. I needed her help, but I didn't want anything to happen to her, so I put her on a regular schedule to make deliveries to people I had been dealing with for a while and could trust. All of the people on Bre'ana's route were people I was in good standing with and they were in good standing with me. She had been doing the route for a few weeks. The buyers got their product and they gave her the money. She had these little labels she put on the money so I knew what stack or bag belonged to which buyer. She's a woman, man, you know. She's big on organization," he chuckled. "When she got home with the money, it was always all there. Nobody ever shorted her. I think she had even built up a little bit of a rapport with everybody. She was all about the business, in and out, no nonsense, just like I taught her. So, no, I don't think anybody set her up with the deliveries. Plus, everybody got their shit. Nobody called me saying she didn't drop off their shit, and when I called around, everybody had made their exchanges with her at their normal times."

"Okay, so do you think it was a jack move? You think they were after the money and took her in the process?" A-town asked him.

"That's definitely a possibility, but it would mean somebody had been watching her to know what days she delivered and where. Hell, they'd have to know that she was doing the shit period because not many people knew it," he explained.

"Aight, so we'll keep that in mind," Lil Nard said. "Write down her schedule for the day she went missing, and we'll retrace her steps again and see what we come up with."

Will did just that, and when Lil Nard and A-town left, he laid back on the couch with his eyes closed, trying to collect himself and gain control over his emotions. He must've sat there two seconds too long because there was a knock at the door.

"Who is it?" he shouted without moving, but there was no response. "Who the fuck is it?" he shouted again, but there was still silence. He jumped up and tried to look out of the peephole, but there was something covering it on the other side of the door. He immediately whipped out his .45 and readied himself for an attack. Snatching the door open, Will stuck the barrel of his pistol into Toya's face.

"What the fuck?!" she shouted.

"Toya, what the fuck are you doing here?" he asked, his gun still drawn on her.

"Heard your girl was missing. I thought you could use some company," she said as she moved to enter the house.

"I don't need your company, Toya. You ain't got the picture yet? I don't want shit to do with you."

"Boy, please! You belong to me. You gone always want this pussy," she rolled her eyes at him.

"Toya, I don't have time for your bullshit," he huffed.

"So open up and let me in. I'll make it quick," she giggled as she batted her fake lashes that were long enough to be wings.

"Do you fucking hear me?! Get the fuck away from my

house and stay the fuck away from me, you insensitive ass, leeching ass bitch! You just couldn't wait for a crack to open in a door to even squeeze through. News flash, Toya! I don't want you anymore! It's over! It's bee over! I'd appreciate it if you leave here, leave me alone, and act like you never knew me."

"But, Will-"

BOOM! CLICK!

Will slammed the door in her face and locked it. He waited for a few seconds and then peeped out the blinds. He watched Toya get into her little green Toyota Corolla with the red hood, light a cigarette with tears rolling down her cheeks, and pull off. He sighed in relief as he leaned back against the door.

"Fuck, man!" he whispered, shaking his head

*   ~   *   ~   *

Two days later, my stomach was touching my back and I just knew death was certain I rolled over on the old dusty sofa when I heard a car pull up to the house and a door open and close. Oh great, I thought to myself. An early morning ass whooping.

Tristian came in smiling, acting like everything about our situation was normal. He sat a large bag on the kitchen counter and shouted to me over his shoulder as he unloaded it.

"Good morning, beautiful. I cooked us breakfast. Are you

hungry?"

I just stared at him through the doorway from the sofa. He was absolutely delusional. What did he think this was? We weren't a happy couple. He had my ass held hostage, chained to the damn heater like a dog. He had cooked me a damn "morning after" breakfast like I was supposed to roll over in his t-shirt smiling with morning breath.

He brought two plates into the living room and placed them on the sofa. They were fully loaded with sausage, bacon, smoked sausages, hash browns, cheese eggs, and pancakes. He came back with butter, salt and pepper, and syrup, and then finally went back to the kitchen and returned with two glasses and a pitcher of orange juice. I just looked at him. As hungry as I was, I wasn't about to eat anything he cooked without him taking a bite first.

"Are you going to eat?" he asked me. "You don't want to let your eggs get cold. Cold eggs is nasty as shit."

He sat down and poured the two glasses of orange juice. I picked up the salt and pepper and began seasoning my eggs and hash browns, trying to buy myself some time. I spread butter across my pancakes and then poured syrup on top, watching out the corner of my eye as Tristian bit into a piece of sausage and then shoved a forkful of hash browns and eggs into his mouth.

I sighed as he chewed, feeling more comfortable about the meal, but still despising his presence. Even though he had brought food today, was sober, and was actually being nice to me, I still did not want to be anywhere around him. I was ready to go home. I missed Will. Hell, I missed the simplest things like a shower and clean clothes. I missed a good night's sleep in a warm bed with my man's arms wrapped around me.

"So how was your night?" he tried to make conversation.

"Tristian, stop playing," I said and rolled my eyes.

"I'm serious. You've got the whole house all to yourself. How do you like it?"

"My waist is hurting from the chain around it," I said as I looked him in the eyes matter-of-factly.

"It's a necessary precaution," he said.

"A necessary precaution? It's cruel and unusual punishment and false imprisonment," I corrected him.

"Well, you were doing the most when you were duct taped, so this is more effective and more efficient."

I just stopped talking. It was obvious he honestly believed that mess. Some kind of way, he had managed to justify all of this in that sick little brain of his. I just pretended to be preoccupied with my food and hoped that he would catch the hint.

"I'll be back tonight," he told me as he packed up when we had finished eating.

"Umm hmm," I said skeptically.

"No, I'm serious. I'm going home to cook us dinner. My

parents are on vacation for the month and your favorite little brother is away at school, so I've got the house pretty much to myself, which is a good thing and a bad thing if you know what I mean."

"I guess," I shrugged. "You should take me home with you."

"Nice try, but I know better," he said as he opened the front door. "I'll be back soon."

Chapter 18

Will got a new letter in the mail every day that week, and everyday Tristian came out to the house and fed me and tried to rape me. I was growing tired of fighting and tired of being beaten. I was tired of being dirty and musty and tired of being in the same clothes. But I refused to give in.

Will was tired of not knowing, tired of the games, tired of missing me. He couldn't take being made a fool of, and the notes were only making it worse.

DONT MESS WITH THE BULL YOUNG MAN

OR YOULL GET THE HORNS

Will recognized the quote from "The Breakfast Club," and it pissed him off.

DONT PUSH IT OR ILL

GIVE YOU A WAR

YOU WON'T BELIEVE

The old "Rambo" quote only pissed him off more. He gave both of the letters to A-town who showed them to Lil Nard.

I MUST BREAK YOU

"Rocky IV," and Will was losing his mind.

YOU AND THAT OTHER DUMMY

BETTER START GETTING MORE

PERSONALLY INVOLVED

WITH YOUR WORK

OR IM GONNA STAB YOU

THROUGH THE HEART

WITH A FUCKING PENCIL

When Will showed Lil Nard and A-town the note, they took it as a direct threat to them as well.

While the notes were coming, Lil Nard and A-town had been conducting a thorough investigation. They had been to every house I had visited the day I was taken and turned up empty-handed. The day they went to the last house, though, their luck changed.

Lil Nard called Will with the news and met him at our apartment while A-town went to handle some drama with his baby momma.

"She was taken at the last house on her route, cuz," he told Will as he sat down on our couch.

"Are you sure? How do you know?"

"I found her chain in the dirt next to the driveway," he said as he pulled my necklace from his jacket pocket. Will's heart dropped. I never took my chain off. I wore it to bed most nights too. Will knew how precious it was to me.

"Oh God," Will whispered as he took the broken chain from Lil Nard.

"A-town found a crackhead who saw somebody wearing a gray jogging suit with the hood over their head snatch Bre and throw her into the back seat of her car and pull off. He couldn't give him any kind of description though because it was dark and he didn't see the person's face," he explained.

"This is some bullshit. This is bullshit! Bullshit!" Will yelled in anger as he paced back and forth.

"Calm down, cuz. You ain't in the hood. Mother fuckers over here gone call them folks on your ass."

"This is bullshit," he whimpered as he plopped down on the couch.

"We gone find her, cuz. Give us a little time. These notes keep coming, the nigga gone slip up and say some shit that'll give his ass away," Lil Nard assured him.

"Man, cuz, I'm gone murk this nigga! This nigga think this shit is a joke. He playing with my mother fucking wife, dawg! This shit ain't no game, bruh!"

The weekend went by without a note, and Will spent it canvassing the neighborhood where I was taken looking for anyone who had seen anything and could give them any information they didn't already have.

* ~ * ~ *

"Bre'ana," Tristian's voice interrupted my sleep. I hadn't even heard him pull up. "Wake up, Bre'ana."

"Ummm," I moaned as I rubbed my eyes. "What?" I opened my eyes and allowed them to focus on Tristian and the man standing next to him. "Kyle?"

"Kyle's going to come guard you," Tristian announced.

"You're in on this too?" I frowned disappointedly.

"He noticed I was gone a lot when he came home and decided he wanted to tag along," Tristian explained.

"How long have you had this chain on her?" Kyle asked as he approached me. "She's got to be bruised and hurting something awful underneath these clothes."

"Believe me, I am," I assured him.

"How could you do this to her?" Kyle turned to Tristian. "You said you kidnapped her because you love her. You're hurting her, Tris. Do you know how heavy this chain is and how bad that metal will hurt her when it wears away this shirt?"

198

"Look, you're worried about the wrong shit. The bitch is fine. If she doesn't move too much, it won't wear away her shirt. She'll be okay."

"Bro, this shit is foul. You're fucked up for this shit," Kyle told him as he shook his head.

"Man, fuck all that. You just keep an eye on the bitch, bro. That's all I need you to do. Can you handle that?"

"Yeah, man. I got you," he said. I just sat there amazed that they were discussing me like I wasn't sitting there.

Tristian left us there, and I made it up in my mind that Kyle was the weak link and he was going to be my way out. He got bored quickly and struck up a conversation with me about school and our families. Tristian had already told his entire family what happened at dinner when I had come home for Christmas, and though they understood his point of view, they had no sympathy for him because of his actions.

Tristian had become smitten with me quite a while before that. Years, in fact. We had grown up together, so the logical thing for us to do would have been for us to date and get married. It had almost been expected of us, especially by Tristian's family because they all knew he was in love with me. It was an embarrassment to him that I had turned him down and begun dating someone else. It was the biggest failure of his life, and something he just couldn't accept no matter what anyone said to him.

His parents had been sympathetic towards him when he had come home telling the story of what happened at dinner until he revealed how disrespectful he had been to Will and everyone else in attendance. Our parents had been friends longer than we had been alive, so his parents were furious when they found out how Tristian had disrespected my parents to the point that my father had put him out of the house.

Kyle told me all of that while we were sitting there talking. He even revealed that Tristian had dozens of pictures of me in a photo album that he kept in the top drawer of his nightstand and at least a dozen more on the walls in his room. Anyone who went in there would've thought we had been dating for years. I was creeped out. Kyle admitted that he hadn't noticed Tristian's behavior change until I went to Atlanta to go to college and no one was hearing from me. Tristian had been walking around on pins and needles. When he had come home from the dinner, though, it was obvious that he had snapped.

Tristian didn't leave the keys to my chains with Kyle, which was smart on his part because I definitely would have finessed Kyle out of that key. But because he didn't have the key, Kyle had to step out of the room while I relieved myself in the bucket in the corner. Everything about my situation pissed Kyle off. He called it inhumane, which was quite accurate. I wasn't in a position to be embarrassed. All I knew was that I had to survive. I had a man to get home to.

When Tristian came back with dinner, Kyle confronted him about the bucket, but Tristian shot the whole argument down. I just shook my head at Kyle, knowing it was no use. Tristian was not going to negotiate anything with either of us. I just ate my baked chicken that lacked seasoning and kept my mouth closed because I was tired of even talking to

Tristian.

When they left that night, I cried and screamed at the top of my lungs. I was over the bullshit and I wanted to go home. I didn't feel like a woman anymore. I felt like an object, a toy that he was putting on a shelf until he was ready to play. At the time, I had no clue that Tristian had been sending letters to Will or that Will had gotten even one step closer to finding me. I just knew that I was stuck and tired of the status quo.

Chapter 19

"Aye, cuz. Y'all ain't came up with nothing else yet?" Will was on the phone with A-town.

"Naw. You got another letter yet?"

"I'm on my way to the mailbox to check now. It's been three or four days since I got the last one."

Pulling the stack of envelopes from the mailbox, he sorted through them until he found another plain white card envelope with no return address on it.

"I got one," he told A-town.

"What it say, cuz?"

Ripping the envelope open, Will snatched the note out and opened it.

IF I EVER, IF I EVER

SEE YOU HERE AGAIN

YOU DIE

JUST LIKE THAT

"Cuz? Cuz! What it say, cuz?" A-town asked, but there was no response. "Cuz! Cuz, what the note say, nigga? Talk to me."

"I know who it is," Will said quietly.

"Who is it? Tell me who it is so we can go get your girl back.

*   ~   *   ~   *

"Kyle, don't leave him here with me. If you leave, take him with you."

"Bitch, you ain't running shit around here. Kyle is going home and I'm spending the night here with you so that we can have some alone time," Tristian said.

"I don't need no alone time with you. I wish I could get you to stay as far away from me as possible," I told him. "Kyle, please stay. Don't leave me here with him. Please."

"What do you mean 'alone time'?" Kyle asked Tristian.

"You know what I mean," he said as he winked at Kyle.

"It doesn't seem to me she wants that kind of attention from you, bro," Kyle told Tristian.

"I don't give a fuck what she wants. She doesn't make any decisions around here."

"Is this why you've been having mysterious bruises and

black eyes?" Kyle frowned. "You've been out here trying to rape Bre'ana?"

"Yes," I told him, "and I keep fighting him off of me, but he won't let it go. He won't leave me alone."

"Tristian, have you lost your damn mind?!"

"Hey!" Tristian shouted. "Don't listen to this bitch and don't lose focus of what we're doing. And, bitch, you shut the fuck up."

"Hell naw, Tris! Are you fucking serious right now? You've been out here trying to rape Bre'ana? Why would you try to violate her like that? Why would you try to take that right to decide from her? No means no, Tristian. If she don't want to fuck you, don't make her. Don't do that to her."

"Kyle, if you don't take your mother fucking ass home! Ole Professor Oglevee lecturing ass. Standing there looking like a fifty question test. Ole five paragraph essay body ass lil boy!"

I just looked at Tristian. He had just checked the shit out of his brother, and his checks were pretty good, but the shit wasn't funny in the midst of this particular conversation. Kyle was just looking at Tristian, trying to figure out why the hell he really felt that moment was appropriate to start a checking war. But then, to a guy from Memphis, anytime was an appropriate time to flame somebody up.

"Tris, man, I ain't with you on this shit. Kicking it here with her at night, guarding her, that shit is cool. You want me to just walk away and let you rape her. I ain't with this shit. You're foul, bro."

"Mane, Kyle, go home, bro! Go home!"

"But, Tristian-"

"Go home and come back in the morning and get me," Tristian instructed him. "I'm cool, bro. I ain't on no funny business. I'll leave her alone tonight."

Kyle gave me an apologetic look, knowing that his brother was lying. I nodded at him reassuringly, letting him know I understood and appreciated him at least trying. I knew it was no use though. If Kyle hadn't gone ahead and left, he would've found himself on the receiving end of Tristian's rage and frustration. I may have been a female, but I was already used to fighting Tristian off. I knew where to hit or kick him to break him down, and I had developed a method to change up my moves so Tristian wouldn't know what to expect. I couldn't ask Kyle to fight my battles for me.

When Kyle left, Tristian jumped straight to it. He placed candles all around the room and lit them while I watched, rolling my eyes.

"I don't suggest you light all of those candles in this dry rotted ass house," I told him. "Plus, you're doing all of that shit for nothing because I'm still not about to do shit with you."

"Oh, you're giving it up tonight," he told me.

"Like hell! I'm not doing shit."

"Shut up and take your pants off."

I just looked at him. Was that shit really supposed to work? Did he really expect me to just shut up and take off my pants?

He sat next to me on the sofa and put his hand on my thigh. My eyes shot darts at him. He moved closer to me in an attempt to kiss me, and I pulled away. He grabbed the back of my head and tried to force me closer to him, but I stuck my hand between us just before his lips met mine. With the other hand, I picked his hand up off of my thigh and threw it to the side. Then I slapped him with one solid lick that sounded off.

"You ain't gone keep fighting me. I'm sick of playing games with your ass," he said as we tussled.

"Get the fuck away from me! Get off of me!" I said as our arms were flinging and flailing everywhere. I was tired and I had no more fight left in me, but my heart just wouldn't let me give up. The tears began to flow as we fought. I was crying and punching, sobbing and swinging. He got tired of the slaps not working and began punching me in my face and stomach, but I still wouldn't give in. I kept telling myself that I belonged to someone, a man who loved me and cherished me, and I had never done wrong by him. I certainly wasn't going to start with Tristian's trifling ass.

"What you crying for? Huh? Why you crying? You're doing this shit to yourself. You're making me beat your ass. If you stop fighting I wouldn't have to hit you. This shit doesn't have to be painful," he said.

My left eye was swelling and I knew my ribs were probably bruised too, but still, I fought back. Suddenly it hit me: Tristian's injury. If he hadn't been injured, he wouldn't have been there at all. He'd be away at school up north. I kicked him as hard as I could in his left leg with my right foot and watched him hit the floor holding his leg. By the look on his face, you would've thought I had kicked him in the balls.

He wailed and screamed as he rolled around on the floor, but I was unmoved. I knew better than to even think that he expected me to have sympathy for him. He rolled on his back and stared at me. When I was certain he wasn't going to move from that spot, I laid down on the sofa with a satisfied look on my face and dozed off.

*   ~   *   ~   *

Will, Lil Nard, and A-town sat at the end of Tristian's street waiting to see Tristian's BMW 745 pull into a driveway. Will didn't know which house was Tristian's, but he knew this was his street because I had shown it to him. When the black car passed them and pulled into the driveway two houses from the corner, they watched closely.

"That's not him," Will told them. "I mean, that's his car, but that's not him getting out of it. It must be his little brother or something."

"Yeah, well, now we know where he lives," A-town told him.

"Yeah. We'll watch the house and see what kind of movement is going on. He'll show up eventually," Lil Nard said.

"What should we do about his kid brother?" A-town asked, itching for some action. "You want us to hem him up?"

"Nah," Will said. "Let him be. If we kidnap his brother he'll know we're here. We'll move in silence until we're ready to work and then catch him off guard just like he did me. I don't want him to even see it coming."

The three of them sat outside all night waiting for Tristian to return but turned up empty-handed. They watched Kyle pull off from the house around eight-thirty and decided to grab a couple of hotel rooms, get a shower and some sleep, and come back later.

"How long we gone be up here, cuz?" A-town asked as he passed a lit blunt to Lil Nard. "Til we catch him?"

"Nah, we'll head back tomorrow and I'll come back by myself. Y'all niggas got kids and shit. I don't wanna keep y'all away too long."

"Mane, cuz, my gal understand. If it was her, she'd want us to be out here doing the same thing," Lil Nard told him as he ran his hand over his afro.

"Well, I ain't got no gal, but y'all know how my baby momma is. She don't give a fuck what a nigga got going on out here, as long as she free on the weekends to shake her ass and get drunk. That's all these bitches think about: turning up and showing out," he scoffed. "I don't care though, because I love my girls and she knows it. That's why it's always some bullshit. Trifling ass bitch be trying to use my babies against me as a bargaining tool or something. If I don't come back to her, I can't see my kids type of shit."

"Cuz, cuz, cuz," Will stopped him. "We know the story, cuz."

"My bad, cuz. Shit just pisses me off. Guess I just needed to vent for a second."

"You good, nigga. We know what's up," Will told him. "And for what it's worth, cuz, you're a great father. Fuck that bitch. Those girls love you, nigga, and you always come through for them. You stay giving them your last. You might as well get custody and keep them yourself because you know she don't give a fuck about them since she ain't getting the dick no more."

"I know, but you see what the fuck I'm out here doing? I can't have my girls around this shit, cuz. And I won't have anybody to watch them when I can't. I can cook a little bit, but I can't put together a whole nutritious meal every day. I don't have a gal like y'all do. And I'll be damned if I feed them fast food every day."

"Hell, the shit she feeding them ain't no better, cuz. Hot dogs and noodles. Beans and weenies. They probably think French fries are vegetables," Lil Nard laughed.

"That shit ain't funny. I take them over Auntie's house every Sunday when she cooks after church. They know what real food is," A-town said.

209

"Well, that's a relief. At least they're not malnutrition."

"Yeah, but like I was saying, I just have to get my girls on the weekends, so I can't really be out here like that, but I don't have a gal to answer to either," he told Will as he was pulling into a parking space in front of the Hilton Memphis and got out.

"Cuz, I can't afford this shit," Lil Nard protested.

"Who said you were praying?" Will asked and then led them inside.

Chapter 20

"What I don't understand is why. Why would this mother fucker actually kidnap her?" Will sat on the edge of the bed in his hotel room with his head in his hands trying to figure out what the fuck was going on.

"Fuck all that, cuz. The fact is that he did. You'll probably never know why because when we catch this nigga it ain't gone be no talking. I'm straight shooting at his bitch ass," A-town told him.

"But for real, cuz, is the nigga that damn delusional?" Lil Nard asked him. "He literally kidnapped her because he wants to be with her and he's mad that she's with you?"

"I can't see any other reason," Will nodded.

"Do you have any kind of knowledge of his mental status? I mean, you have to think about the fact that he's already kidnapped her. What is his ultimate intention behind this?" Lil Nard asked as he rolled a blunt.

"What do you mean 'his ultimate intention'?" Will frowned.

"Where is this going? He can't possibly be planning to just kidnap her and hold her hostage forever. What is it that he wants? What is he trying to do?"

"Well, it's obviously not motivated by money. His family has plenty of money, and he hasn't sent any kind of ransom letter. He doesn't even know anyone knows he took her," Will reminded them.

"I doubt this has anything to do with money anyway. If that was the case, he could have just robbed her and sent her about her way," A-town explained. "Do you think he'd try to rape her? I mean, she's beautiful and he's obviously had his eye on her for years."

"He's right," Lil Nard said as he lit the blunt he had finished rolling and passed it to Will. "And if he did that, he might even kill her and try to dispose of the body to get rid of the evidence."

"I hope the nigga ain't that damn crazy, but you never know. Shit, it's like y'all said. He done already kidnapped her, so who knows how far he'll actually go. That only makes this shit that much more urgent," Will told them. "Bre'ana can hold her own. I know that for sure. But I don't trust this mother fucker, and I don't want her fighting him forever. I mean, her hands are decent. I saw her beat a bitch in the club, and when Toya and her little friends tried to jump her, she still held her own. But this is a grown man, and there's no telling who's helping him and what they're doing to her."

"You're right, so we have to find this nigga before he goes too far or before Bre'ana gives up," A-town told him.

"Yeah, G. I ain't having that shit. Y'all catch a couple of hours of sleep and then we'll go see if we can catch see if we can catch any action again at the nigga's house," Will told them as he got up and went to the doctor.

* ~ * ~ *

"Ugh! Are you still here?" I asked when I rolled over and saw Tristian laying on the floor next to the couch. He had been watching me sleep which creeped me the fuck out. I was beyond annoyed by his presence and I was tempted to kick him in his face while he was laying there on the floor.

"Of course, Cinderella. Your Prince Charming is always by your side," was his response. I scoffed, rolled my eyes, and sat up on the couch.

"Bruh, what time is it and when is Kyle coming back? I'm sick of looking at you."

"Kyle comes back when I tell him to come back. Right now, you need to focus on what I have for you," he told me.

"Oh, you don't have shit for me. I don't want shit you have except a key to this chain. You can miss me with all your other bullshit because I'm dodging it like a matador."

"You know what? You're putting on this hard shell like a Ninja Turtle, talking all this shit, when you know I know you. This ain't you, Bre. You're a sweet, kind-hearted, quiet, patient person. Stop with the hard act. It ain't cute."

"I don't care if it's cute or not I'm not trying to impress you. I don't give a fuck what you think about me. All I give a fuck about right now is getting the hell out of this house and the fuck away from you. Now where the food at?"

At that moment, Kyle walked in with a big bag from McDonald's. If I had been able to reach him, I would've tackled him for the bag. Since I was chained to a heater across the room, I just sat there. I knew Kyle was going to make sure I was fed, so I had nothing to worry about since he was back.

"Finally! Shit!" I sighed heavily.

"Damn! Did you miss me?" he laughed.

"Mane, come and get your brother, dawg," I told him as he handed me two sausage, egg, and cheese McGriddles and two hash browns.

"Naw, he's your issue. That's your problem to solve," he told me. "You like hot chocolate, right?" He handed me a steaming cup.

"God! Thank you, Kyle. Thank you so much."

"What the fuck are you thanking him for? Hell, he spent my money on the damn food. Gimme the damn bag, man," Tristian said and snatched the bag from his brother.

"Well, at least he actually gives me the damn food. You have the money, don't buy me food, don't feed me, and generally don't give a fuck about my well-being. All you're concerned about is getting your way and getting some ass. Ole sorry ass trick," I said and rolled my eyes. "Can you take your food to go? I'm sick of your ass. Bye, bitch!"

"Bitch, shut the fuck up!" he said and then slapped me so hard I dropped my food. Cup still in my hand, I popped the top off and tossed all of the contents into his face and enjoyed the scream he released.

"That's what the fuck you get!" Kyle fussed at him. "I can't believe you're in here putting your hands on her. I have no sympathy for you."

"Shut up and give me some napkins or something to get this shit out of my eyes," he yelled at Kyle. "The shit is burning."

I sat on the sofa eating a McGriddle and watching the show. My cheek was still stinging from the slap, but I was enjoying his suffering so much that I didn't even notice my own pain. Kyle handed me his bottled water to drink with my food while Tristian was busy clearing whipped cream and hot chocolate from his eyes.

* ~ * ~ *

"Cuz, if you need us for anything, let us know," A-town told Will the next morning when they arrived back in Atlanta. They had staked out Tristian's house again the following evening but had only seen Kyle returning to the house again. Will had taken Lil Nard and A-town back home as promised.

Will was upset when he stepped back into our house without me on his arm. The house seemed especially empty and his footsteps seemed to echo on the carpet. He ran himself a bath, poured himself a Remy and Coke, and sat in the tub with the Jacuzzi jets on, trying not to allow himself to cry. The tears came anyway, and he hated his tears. He hated the pain and helplessness that he was feeling. When he went to bed that night, he fell asleep hugging my pillow, praying that God sends me back to him.

Waking up alone the next morning, Will decided to go back to Memphis and not leave until he figured out where I was and had me securely in his possession. He packed suitcases in the back of the Escalade and even packed a bag for me as well, and hit the road back to Tennessee.

When he checked back into the Hilton Memphis, he sat in his hotel room going over all of the information he had already acquired and trying to figure out what he had missed or done wrong. He realized he had only sat in front of Tristian's house at night. He hadn't observed any activity during the middle of the day. He decided to spend the rest of the day at the hotel and then spend the next day watching Tristian's house.

It was six the next morning when Will headed out to sit in front of Tristian's house. Tristian's car was still in the driveway, so he knew he hadn't missed anything. He just didn't know how wrong he was with that assumption, but he realized that when he saw my truck pull into the driveway and park behind Tristian's BMW at about nine-thirty.

Will sat straight up in the front seat of the Escalade with his face twisted into a deep, confused frown, but as soon as the driver's door opened, that confusion turned into a blazing anger. It was like a slap in the face to Will to see Tristian driving my truck like it was his or even as though he had permission to be behind the wheel of my car.

A series of thoughts ran through Will's mind as he fought

the urge to jump out and strangle Tristian until he told him where I was. For a brief second, he wondered if I had actually run away with my childhood friend and he was driving my car with both my knowledge and my permission. The next second, he put it completely out of his mind by remembering the smile in my eyes every time I saw him and in my voice every time he called. Watching Tristian go into the house and close the door, he wondered if he had just returned from a night of passionate love-making with me, and then within the next instance, wondered if he had violated me by raping me yet. That feeling was immediately followed and over-powered by the realization that he could just as possibly be returning from murdering me and dumping my mutilated, lifeless body in some stream or open field.

Will punched the steering wheel, accidentally blowing the horn. He looked around to see if anyone had noticed, but although it was a relatively quiet neighborhood and car horns were not the norm, everyone was at school and at work, so the car horn went unnoticed.

"I'm gone kill this nigga," Will whispered to himself through gritted teeth. "First he kidnaps my wife, and now he's riding around in my baby's shit like it's cool! He's bold as hell. If I had let Bre's parents file that missing person report, they would've busted his ass by now. But that's okay because there's a special place in hell for sick ass mother fuckers like that. I'm going to off his ass when I figure out what the fuck is going on so he can lay in the burning bed he's made. He gone be the one missing."

Will sat posted up in the truck for hours and watched the house. Kyle left and came back a couple of times, but Tristian remained unseen. Will wrote down everything he observed in a notebook so that nothing was overlooked or forgotten.

Around eight that evening, Will heard the engine turn over in my truck. He sat up in his seat after hours of inactivity and watched Tristian hop into the driver's seat and pull off.

It was dark outside. Will watched my truck pass him and then looked in the rear view mirror to watch my tail lights pull to the stop sign at the end of the street and then turn left. Then he cranked up his truck and followed Tristian as he got onto I-240 and then floored it. Will kept up with him for a few miles, but as he neared the Wolfchase Mall, Will decided to fall back.

*   ~   *   ~   *

Forty-five minutes later, Tristian pulled back up to the house where I was wasting away. I had enjoyed being alone in the house the night before as much as I could, but it didn't take away from the fact that I was tired of being there. My sadness had turned into fear and anger. I was afraid of Tristian and what he was capable of. I was angry with Will because he hadn't found me yet. I didn't have time to deal with my emotions, though, because I was dealing with Tristian standing in front of me in the flesh.

I had officially lost track of the days and how long I had been there. I did know that I had been in the same clothes and underwear for at least three weeks and I felt filthy. I also knew that if Tristian didn't let me go soon he was going to be buying feminine hygiene products at the grocery store too. I had already been forced to lows I could never have imagined, but I refused to allow Tristian to completely dehumanize me. I was a woman before anything else, and if he couldn't understand that, I'd just choke his ass out every time I saw him until he gained some comprehension.

"Where the food at, Tristian?" I asked him, not even attempting to hide my annoyance.

"I didn't bring any," he said bluntly.

"What do you mean you didn't bring any? How the fuck am I supposed to survive?"

"Fuck you! You ain't giving me no pussy, so I ain't giving you no food."

"So I'm just supposed to sit here and die?"

"You don't have to. You could spread your legs and then I'd feed you," he said and shrugged his shoulders.

"You a nasty ass mother fucker. You know that? You've had me locked up in this shack for weeks. I haven't had a bath I haven't had no tissue to wipe my ass when I shit. But your nasty ass is still trying to stick your dick up in my unwashed pussy. I'm musty. My breath smells like shit. My hair is nappy and in desperate need of a perm. I've sweated and bled all over these clothes, and your trifling ass is still trying to be dick deep in the middle of this mess. What the fuck is wrong with you, Tristian? Seriously. What the fuck is wrong with you?" I crossed my arms over my chest. "There aren't enough rich, prissy white girls up there at that school chasing after you? Hell, I'm sure the black girls are after you too. You don't want them, though. You just have to have the one person who ain't studying your ass even a bit more than the man on the moon. What the fuck is wrong with you?"

"You're what's wrong with me," he said.

"Care to elaborate?" I asked him.

"You're what's wrong with me. You're my problem," he sighed and sat down on the opposite end of the sofa. "You left and went to school in Atlanta instead of going to Harvard, Yale, or Princeton like you were supposed to. You ran off with this random guy who is nowhere near being in the same hemisphere as your league…and you were happy," he admitted, the hurt and defeat evident in his voice. "You were happy, and you didn't even think about me or how I was going to feel about it. I felt pushed to the side, abandoned, ignored, worthless. I was hurt, Bre'ana. I still am," he said as he looked up into my eyes. "You left and didn't even come home to visit. You ran off and got your own life while I was still holding on to the possibility of me and you."

"And that justifies this? All of this, Tristian?" I asked as I spread my arms for emphasis. "You kidnapped me. You've been beating me. You're barely feeding me. I'm losing weight daily. And to make it worse, you've been trying to force me to have sex with you. If I ever was going to love you, do you think I could love you behind this?"

"You won't have a choice," he said, a sudden change washing over his face, "because you're stuck with me."

220

With that, he stood up, went to the corner, grabbed the bucket I had been relieving myself in, and took it out the back door to dump it. I had never seen someone so stubborn. I understood his hurt, but it in no way justified what he had done or what he was doing. And no matter how hurt he claimed to be, he was inflicting that hurt onto me, but ten times worse. A broken heart is one thing, but to physically injure me was taking it to another level. I sucked up any drop of sympathy or understanding I had for him and slid my poker face back into position. If he wanted to keep this up, we could keep going with it, but the one thing I was not going to do was give up.

Chapter 21

"Cuz, where you been at?"

"Out here looking for my girl, man. I've been in Memphis for a couple of days. You heard anything?"

"Not really. Is she supposed to be up this way?" Big Bang's voice boomed in Will's ear.

"Yeah. I figured out who snatched her, but I gotta find out where the fuck he got her held up."

"I might have something for you. Come through here in about an hour," he said.

When Will pulled into Big Bang's driveway, he had a feeling that everything was going to be okay. Something deep down inside told him that something positive was going to come from this visit. As down as his spirits had been, he had tried his best to be optimistic about the situation. Any little glimmer of hope would help him at this point.

"What's up, my nigga?" Goose greeted him at the door. "Come on in here. I found the nigga for you."

"Found who?" Will frowned, confused.

"The white boy. You were looking for the white boy,

right?"

"Well, yeah," Will said as he stepped through the doorway, "but how'd you-" Will's voice trailed off. He couldn't believe his eyes He looked back and forth between Big Bang and Goose who were both standing over a white man in his mid-fifties balled up on the floor with his hands attempting to cover his head. He was shivering in fear and on the verge of tears.

"Goose, Bang, man, y'all let me go. I ain't did nothing. I paid my debt. Goose, I paid you, man. I paid you," the man whined.

"Y'all, this ain't the guy I was looking for," Will told them.

"Yes, it is," Big Bang assured Will. "Shut up, fool!" he yelled at the crying man on the floor. "This ain't about no money. Get your ass up off the floor before I punch you again."

"W-what you got me over here for then, Bang? Why y'all jumping on me for?" he asked as he scraped himself up off the floor.

"We beat your ass because you didn't bring your ass on when we told you to," Goose told him. "If you had just got your ass in the truck like we said, we wouldn't have touched you, but you took off running and I had to chase you. Therefore, you got your ass beat."

"Man, I didn't know what was going on," he tried to explain.

"You don't need to know what's going on. You just need to do as you're told if you don't want me to box your ass. Sit down on the couch before I punch you again," Goose told him.

"Y'all quit threatening him. Who is this dude and why do y'all have him here?" Will asked.

"Tell him what you told us the other day," Big Bang instructed the man.

"Tell him what? What did I tell y'all?" he asked.

"You came over here two or three nights ago. Band and I were sitting here counting money and bagging up weed. Remember?" Goose jogged his memory.

"Yeah, faintly," he nodded.

"You were rambling about not being able to sleep, something about some screaming you were hearing," Bang said.

"Yeah, man," the guy said as he sat up on the couch. "I came over here trying to get some shit to help me sleep because I keep hearing this crying and screaming at night out in the county where I go hunting."

"You go hunting?" Will frowned.

"Yeah, yeah. It's springtime, so the weather is nice. I drive out to Fayette County to my parents' old house and sleep there because I don't have anywhere else to go. I hunt a bit while I'm out there."

"If that's the case, why don't you live out there then?" Goose asked. "You're out here sleeping in your car and shit."

"The house is paid for, but there isn't any electricity on the inside of it. I can't afford the utilities. I can barely keep gas in my truck. My social security check goes there, so I have to drive out there anyway," he shrugged. "It's convenient for the most part. It's a place to store my stuff and lay my head, but when it's too hot or too cold outside, I'm better off sleeping in the truck because the house is drafty."

"I'm sorry," Will interrupted. "What does this have to do with me?"

"My bad, cuz. I was just curious. Tell him what you were telling us about the crying and shit," Goose said.

"So I've been going out there a couple of days a week to catch some sleep. You know, when I go on a binge, I can sense when my body is about to crash, so I head out there to the house so that I can sleep it off in peace without anyone bothering me because it's no telling how long I'm going to be asleep and I'm tired of mother fuckers thinking I'm dead or done overdosed," he ranted. He looked around and saw the impatience on everyone's face and got to the point. "I'm sorry. So, for the past couple of weeks, when I go out there I keep hearing these screams and a woman crying. I can't figure out for the life of me where it's coming from, but it's close enough that I can hear it, but far enough away that I can't find it. I mean, it's not like I go looking for it either," he shrugged his shoulders.

"So you think this has something to do with me how?" Will asked Big Bang.

"Well, I wasn't for certain, but I definitely thought it was worth mentioning when you said you were up here looking for her. Fayette County isn't but a few minutes past the city limits."

"I feel you, but there's a very small chance that the woman he hears screaming is my girlfriend. I could go out there investigating and stumble upon some shit I don't want no parts of. I'll fuck around and come up missing too," Will explained to him.

"We weren't suggesting that you should go out there investigating and hit, Sherlock. We just thought that this information should be something comes up that makes it relevant," Goose explained. "No case is ever solved without a bunch of different factors coming together to paint the entire picture. As irrelevant as the shit he's saying may sound, listen to him because it may end up being an essential fragment of information at a later time."

"I got you. I understand," Will told them. "I'll write it in my notes in case I need it later."

Will smoked a blunt with Big Bang and Goose after the man left and then headed back to the hotel to grab a drink at the bar. He was frustrated because he knew he was missing something somewhere along the way...but he also knew that Goose was right.

The answer came to him as he sat posted in front of Tristian's house an hour later.

"I need to get into the house and look around," he told himself. "The next time they both leave I'm going to snoop around and see what I can come up with."

When Tristian and Kyle both left the house at the same time that evening, Will pounced on the opportunity and seized the moment. He pulled his truck directly across the street from Tristian's house and jumped out. Part of him was worried that someone would see him and call the police, but he put that thought out of his head when he considered how long he had been parked on that street without raising any suspicions.

Walking along the side of the house, he peeked into each window he passed, trying to get a feel for the layout of the inside of the house. He unlatched the back gate, walked in, and closed it behind himself. The entire neighborhood had been crime-free since the first moment he turned onto the street. He had watched the residents come and go at the same time every single day as if they were set on the same timers as their porch lights. They suspected nothing and expected nothing.

Will peered through the patio door at the newly remodeled kitchen and the beautiful living room just past it. Searching the far wall, his eyes fell on the alarm system keypad. The alarm hadn't been set. To Will, that meant two things: he could get in undetected and he had to be quick because someone was likely returning soon. All of this was not helped by the fact that he had no clue what he was actually looking for. He was just looking for something, anything that could point him in the right direction.

The patio door had been left unlocked, which made Will leery. Even in that neighborhood, it was still Memphis. Who left a door unlocked while they were gone? He pulled a pair of latex gloves from his jacket pocket and put them on before sliding the glass door back. He went straight to the fridge, found two packs of lunch meat, and sat them on the counter. Then he looked around.

There was nothing abnormal about the house. There were pictures in the living room, mail on the side table, keys hanging by the door. He couldn't find anything helpful, so he headed upstairs because he knew his best chance of finding any kind of information would be in Tristian's bedroom.

Stepping lightly up the stairs, Will was cautious to stay alert and light on his feet in case anything happened. Opening the first door in the hall, Will knew immediately that he was in Kyle's room, though he didn't know Kyle's name. Kyle had been a basketball star in middle school and it had led him all the way to the varsity basketball team at his high school. He had photos and trophies lining the walls of his bedroom.

Stepping out and closing the door, he walked down the hall and opened the next door, Tristian's room. It was obvious. Will's eyes got big as he entered the room. My eyes lured him inside and my lips blew him kisses.

"This mother fucker is sick," Will whispered to himself as he looked around at all of the photos of me in different poses and positions on Tristian's wall. "Why the fuck does he have all of these pictures of my girl on his wall when they were never even together?" he asked himself with a disgusted frown plastered across his face.

Will rambled through the drawers on Tristian's desk, looking for any slip of paper with an address written on it or any kind of information that would help him find me. Nothing. Will told himself that wherever this place was, Tristian either didn't know the address or didn't need it written down, and Will was leaning towards the latter.

Will may not have been the best looking guy to most females, and he certainly didn't look appealing to my parents and anyone in their circle, but I had discovered very early in our relationship that he was a master at critical thinking. There was no box that he couldn't think outside of, no puzzle that he couldn't piece together. The most minute details meant the absolute most to Will because he realized that though the largest pieces gave you the most information and pushed you further ahead in the game, they were few and far between. Any criminal- whether amateur or professional- has two goals to commit their crime and to get away with it. Nobody who has put any real thought into their crime is going to make a big, obvious mistake or leave an important clue in plain sight or in a place with easy access. This situation was no different.

Will hadn't been home, but the letters had continued to come. Even if Will hadn't figured out who was responsible for my abduction with the last letter he had opened, he would've deciphered it eventually because every single letter got more and more brazen with its hint as if Tristian was urging him to come and find me.

As he rambled through Tristian's desk though, Will found

the magazines and newspapers Tristian had been clipping the letters from for the notes, and even the scissors he had used to cut them out. Everything inside of Will wanted to destroy that whole fucking bedroom, but he knew he couldn't because he didn't want anyone to know he had been there. He simply continued to search.

He searched relentlessly through the drawers and stacks of papers but came up empty-handed. He was frustrated and disappointed.

Turning around to face the bookshelf behind the desk, Will came face-to-face with a framed photo that stood out from the rest. All of the other photos were of me or Tristian's family. This photo was of Tristian as a young boy. It appeared to have been taken on a farm. Tristian stood there in the sunlight smiling from ear to ear with an older man- assumedly his grandfather- at his side with his arm around Tristian's shoulder.

Will examined the details of the picture. The front of the house was pictured clearly, but there were no numbers on the building. There was a small green car, possibly a Toyota Tercel, parked next to an old Ford pick-up in the yard. It was dark, so Will wasn't sure, but he believed he could make out the license plate on the back of the truck. He tucked the picture securely inside of his jacket, closed the desk drawers, and headed out the same way he had come in. Seeing that there was no dog inside the house, he put the lunch meat back into the fridge, slipped back out of the patio door, and drove off into the night.

Chapter 22

Will operated that night on pure adrenaline. When he made it back to his hotel room, he immediately pulled out his laptop to do some research. He researched Tristian's family members and property they owned but didn't locate anything nearby from the records he found. He researched old and foreclosed properties for sale and still turned up empty-handed.

By the time the sun came peeking through the curtains into the room, Will was barely able to keep his eyes open. He was still frustrated, but that frustration was over-powered by his hope that had reflourished after finding the picture.

"Malcolm," he said as he made a phone call. "It's Will. Yeah, yeah. Look, man. I need a huge favor.

"No favor is too big for you, bruh. You know that," Malcolm said on the other end of the line. Malcolm had once been one of Will's customers. Will had saved his life one night when he had stumbled upon another dealer with the hole of his .45 to Malcolm's head threatening to blow his noodles all over the alley they were in if he didn't pay up on his debt. Malcolm didn't have the money and was just getting off work, having been blind-sided behind the restaurant he worked at. He had been one of Will's customers for years, and though he often got into debt, he always paid up. Will paid the gun-wielding dealer for Malcolm and told Malcolm to go home and pay him later. He didn't see Malcolm for four months, but when he did, Malcolm paid him the four g's he owed him plus an extra G as interest and a thank you gift.

"I need you to run a tag for me," Will told him.

"Sure. I don't go in until this evening, but I got you. What's the tag?" Malcolm had been clean for over three years and was approaching his two-year anniversary at the DMV. Will read him the tag on the truck in the photograph and gave him a description of the truck. "Any particular information you're looking for?"

"Just a name and address, but give me whatever you can come up with," Will told him as he ran his fingers through his dreadlocks.

"Okay. Cool. I'll hit you back around five-thirty or six o'clock when I go on break. I'll have the information for you then," he assured him.

"Cool, and thanks again, man," Will said as he stood up and looked at the digital alarm clock on the side table. It was eight twenty-seven in the morning.

"No problem, man. Anytime you need me just hit me up," Malcolm said before hanging up.

"Bae," Will whispered as he closed the blinds and curtains, "I'm going to lay down until Malcolm calls me back. Just hold tight for me, baby. I'm coming. I'm coming."

*   ~   *   ~   *

I was holding on, alright. Holding on tight as hell to Tristian's neck. I was trying to choke the life out of him after I had once again gotten him in my clutches while he was trying to dip in another man's cookie jar. At that exact moment that Will was drawing the curtains and climbing under the covers, I was just getting up and had found Tristian, who had spent the night at the house again, standing over me with his dick not even a half an inch from my nose.

"Suck it," was the only thing he said before he tried to shove it in my mouth.

I must've grabbed that thing with a grip of death and refused to let it go. Tristian released the highest pitched wail I had ever heard from a man. It sounded like a wounded cat being startled and then thrown into a tub of water. I squeezed it as hard as I could until he punched me in the face, forcing me to release my grip.

"Oh God!" he huffed in agony. "Bitch, I'm gone kill you. I'm gone kill you."

"Yeah, whatever, mother fucker," I smirked. "Good morning to you too."

"You think this shit is funny? I'm going to smack that smirk right off your face," he threatened me, still rolling on the floor holding his wounded manhood.

"You'd have to get up off the floor first, ass hole," I said and rolled my eyes at him. His pride was hurt and he was burning with anger. His eyes narrowed as I laughed at him and shook my head, and I suddenly found myself pressed against the back of the sofa with Tristian's hands around my throat.

Maybe some people would panic in that situation. The fear of death is very real for most people. I felt like I had already seen death, and I certainly felt like I smelled like it. But as close to death I felt like I may have been at that moment, I wasn't dead yet. I may have been on the Grim Reaper's doorstep, but I hadn't knocked on the door yet. As long as I had one singular puff of breath left in my body, I was going to fight. I mentally forced everything to slow down and focused directly on the most important issue: Tristian's hands around my throat. Not my inability to breathe, the possibility that I could lose consciousness, or even his dick dangling over my lap. My biggest concern was getting him the fuck off of me.

My mind noted all of his vulnerable spots in two seconds, and then I sprang into action. One swift kick to his already injured groin got him off of me, and a punch to his stomach and then his nose took him down. I jumped on top of him on the floor and wrapped my hands tight around his throat with every intention of taking his life.

Forget the fact that I had known him all my life. Fuck the close-knit personal and business relationships our parents had developed. Fuck his hopes and dreams of one day wedding me. I forgot all about my aspirations of becoming a world-re-nown chemical engineer. Everything about life in the civilized world went out the window. At that moment, I was relentless-ly homicidal and desperate to survive, and I knew that my survival was dependent upon his death.

But my survival was also dependent on his survival as

well. His phone was in the car. The key to my chain was with Kyle. If Tristian didn't call Kyle, he wouldn't come. It would be a few days before Kyle would become suspicious of Tristiann not answering the phone and come to check on us. I didn't have a few days. I already hadn't eaten in almost a week. A few more days would likely cause my body to begin shutting down. I was already so malnutrition that my cycle hadn't even peeked its head around a corner. That said enough to me.

Tristian didn't possess the self-control I did. He was in such a state of shock that he hadn't even attempted to fight back. The state of panic had caused his air supply to be even shorter than it would have been had he not panicked. He was slipping away right in front of me, and I still had no intention of letting up.

"Bre'ana!"

I looked up to see Kyle standing in the doorway in shock.

"Bre'ana, let him go. Let him go," he whispered. I looked down at Tristian and back up at Kyle whose fear was written across his face. I look back down at Tristian and released my grip.

"Get out, Tristian," I said in a low tone. He just sat on the floor rubbing his neck and trying to get reaccustomed to having air in his lungs. "Get, up, Tristian. Leave. Now."

"You can't put me out. This is my folks' house," he tried to protest.

"Tris, no offense, but I think it's best that you leave, bro. She would've killed you if I hadn't come in just now. You should probably leave her the fuck alone for a minute," Kyle advised him. Tristian looked back and forth between us and then surrendered. Kyle helped him up from the floor and to the door. "Go home, bro," he told him. He turned to me and said, "Bre'ana… I… I don't even know what to say right now. I'm sorry you're being put through any of this, but, please, don't kill him. He's an asshole. Okay? We both know it. But don't kill him."

"Kyle, you have no idea what I go through when you're not here, what he was doing to me before you found out, what he's going to do every time he comes out here. To make matters worse, you've witnessed some of it and you're still helping him. You've been much nicer to me than him, I admit, but you're still his accomplice all the same. Hell, you have the key to my chains. If you really gave a fuck, Kyle, you'd let me out of here before I starve to death or your brother beats me to death." I curled back up on the sofa in a fetal position and moved the chains around so that they weren't rubbing against the sores they had worn into my skin.

"I'm sorry, Bre. I really am no better than him. My brother loves you. He's obsessed. He's infatuated with you. He's been crazy about you since you guys were little kids. I understand how he feels, even though I don't condone his behavior. Here," he said as he approached me. "I bought you this blanket. I know it gets a little chilly out here at night," he said and put the blanket over me. "Try to get some sleep. I'll be back soon to check on you."

"Yeah. Get some sleep with these open sores and an empty

stomach. No problem," I said sarcastically, rolled my eyes, and turned my back to him.

"I'm sorry, Bre," he whispered before the door clicked shut.

Chapter 23

While I was sitting there trying to calm myself down after almost committing my first murder, Will was flopping in the bed like a fish out of water, trying to get comfortable enough to doze off. I was trying my best not to think of him, knowing that it would get my emotions in an uproar, and yet, all he could think of was me. I was in his thoughts, in his dreams, and in his prayers. I was a beautiful dream turned into a vicious, devastating nightmare that wouldn't allow him to function at all until it was resolved.

I was wishing that I at least had that old chemistry book that Mr. Greer had let me borrow all of those years ago during the summer break when I first met Will. It would have at least given me something to do to occupy my mind. I never thought I could ever miss school, but I missed both school and my textbooks. I missed my bed and my apartment. I missed living life. I missed my innocence. I missed being able to do anything, not just the illegal shit and making money, but the legal, smart, calm shit too. I missed learning and going to school, watching TV with my head on Will's lap, dancing in the living room and singing in the kitchen. At that moment, as much as I was laying there trying not to think about it, I would have given anything to get it back.

Will finally dozed off around eleven and might as well have been considered unconscious once he finally fell asleep. My poor baby. He must've run himself out of fuel and out of fumes too. He slept soundly until five-forty when Maurice's call sent his phone vibrating across the nightstand playing loud rap music. Rolling over, he felt around for the phone and sat straight up in the bed when he looked at the screen.

"Maurice, what's up, man?" he answered groggily.

"I got that information you asked me for. Got a pen and paper ready?" Maurice asked.

"Yeah. Yeah. Go ahead," Will told him as he grabbed the ink pen and notepad on the nightstand.

"Okay, so the tag you gave me belongs to a red 1967 Ford Ranger that was registered to Bobby Earl Dewitt. The last renewal on the registration was in 1996," he told him.

"Was there an address on the registration information?"

Maurice read Will the only address that had ever been listed on the registration and then cleared his throat.

"Look, Will. I don't know what you need this information for and I never ask you any questions. I can tell whatever it is, it's urgent. Just be careful, man. That's all I got to say. Just be careful."

"I will, Maurice. I promise. And thank you again," Will said and then hung up. He pulled the framed picture he had stolen from Tristian's bookshelf out of the nightstand drawer. "Bobby Earl Dewitt," he repeated while staring at Tristian's grandfather. "I'm about to send your grandson to join you, old man. He'll be seeing you real soon."

The alarm clock read five fifty-eight when Will rose from the bed. He was well-rested, despite the nightmares and tossing and turning. He was calm and at peace with what he knew he was about to do. We were just kids, but we were wildly in love. There was nothing we wouldn't do for each other. There was no one without the other.

Stepping into the first shower he had taken in three days, he closed his eyes and allowed the hot water to calm him even more. His first thought was a wish that he had showered before he had laid down, realizing that the warm water would have helped him sleep. His second thought was the beginning of a plan formulation. But as quickly as he began mapping out the plan, he scratched the entire thing off of his mental notepad. There was no plan to formulate, no preparation to make. This was love and war. All that was required at that moment was pure animalistic instinct, thoughtless indiscretion, and relentless savagery.

He sifted through the clothes he had packed and picked out a pair of sweatpants and a matching jacket and t-shirt. The hair band snapped into place as Will secured his dreads in a ponytail to prepare for a possible fight. He knew nothing would be easy and I was no prize to be won. I was a woman, a human being, and the love of his life, and I needed to be rescued at all costs before his mission became a recovery.

Will put on three holsters in the hotel room and slid the weapons into them when he made it to the car. A .45, a .40, and a .38. Will had always taught me the importance of not only knowing my weapon but knowing the differences in my weapons. The .40 and the .45 packed more power and left bigger holes. They were weapons with intentions to kill or seriously injure. As reliable as I would believe them to be, with an automatic there is always the possibility that it might jam. In critical moments it's always important to remember that revolvers never jam. Hence, the .38. Revolvers only hold and shoot up to a maximum of six bullets, but they are reliable. If I ever had to use my revolver, the only thing I needed to remember was how many bullets my gun held and to make each shot count. The .38 was also lighter than the bigger guns, so it was easier to conceal in less suspecting places, like an ankle- where Will wore his,- or a thigh- where I wore mine.

Will programmed the address in the GPS in his truck and waited as it calculated a route. It was a forty-eight minute trip to the address in Fayette County, Tennessee. He crept slowly past Tristian's house, checking the driveway. No one was home. He knew exactly where they both were.

*　～　*　～　*

With the plush blanket to cover me, I had actually gotten a bit of sleep while Kyle and Tristian were gone. I still had not eaten, and because there was nothing coming into my body, it had been slow putting anything out. Where it had once taken me only a couple of days to fill the waste bucket Tristian had provided me, the bucket had now been sitting in the corner for over a week and was just then almost full. The smell was horrid, but their lazy asses hadn't dumped the waste. Flies were beginning to buzz around it and I wouldn't have been surprised to see maggots inside of it either.

I kept telling myself that this was not life. This wasn't real. None of this had really happened to me. But when I tried to roll over and the chain wrapped tighter around my waist,

I couldn't psyche myself out about it anymore. My life really was in danger, and every day I spent there I was just that much closer to losing my battle. I knew Will was looking for me, but I also had lost hope that he would ever find me. I had been there too long, and as determined as I knew Will was to find me, he also hadn't heard from me and probably assumed I was dead. A person will only search for so long before they begin to believe there's nothing there to find.

I looked around at the empty ass living room. I was going to die here. That's what I told myself. I hadn't been married yet, and I hadn't gotten my first job. I hadn't felt the miracle of having a little life growing inside of me or the accomplishment of giving birth to a miniature replica of me and the man I loved. I hadn't graduated from college or bought my first house. I would lose my life here in this dilapidated shack and my life would be left incomplete and unaccomplished. I had mastered twerking on top of tables in heels while I was drunk and cooking dope like I was a top chef, but I hadn't done anything that actually meant something or helped someone. My parents would be left with nothing to smile about or be proud of me for. Their one and only child would become their greatest disappointment, their biggest failure.

Tristian came barging into the house with Kyle at his heels, rambling and ranting. I rolled my eyes at them, pissed that they had even returned and annoyed that they were empty-handed. As strong-minded as I was, I could tell that I was fading physically. My stomach no longer growled; it just ached with random sharp pains. I was constantly tired, no matter how much I slept. My head hurt and my lips and eyes were dry. I was trying my best not to give up mentally, but my body's physical state wasn't making that easy at all.

"I'm serious, Tris," Kyle was fussing. "I'm not going to keep doing this with you. This shit is wrong, and it's fucking illegal. If she tells, we can go to jail for a very long time. Look at me. Do I look like I could survive in jail?"

"Your ability to survive is not determined by your appearance," Tristian told him. "It's determined by your desire to survive and your physical capabilities. Anyway, I'm not trying to go to jail, so you can get that thought out of your head. You see this?" he asked as he picked up my chain, showing Kyle. "She ain't going nowhere, bro. Who is she going to tell? There's no one else here. No one knows where we are. She's locked up securely. We're good."

"First of all, you can stop trying to run these mind games on me with your Freudian theories and shit. That reverse psychology shit does not work on me. Second, just because no one knows where she is right now doesn't mean that no one is looking for her or no one will find out. If anybody finds out you kidnapped her or where she is, we're both fucked. Your drug me into this shit with you, and I let you. If I get into any kind of bullshit because of this, I'll never forgive you, Tristian," Kyle told him. I was sitting there silently observing the discussion, so engulfed by it that I may as well have had a bag of popcorn and a soda to enjoy with the show.

"How would anybody find out where she is? Nobody has lived here in years. No one even knows who took her."

"Because you're stupid. I know you. You like to torture people. You've talked so much shit about her boyfriend I wouldn't be surprised if you've been taunting him too."

"Taunting him how, Kyle?"

"I don't know. Any of the little stupid tricks that pop up in that demented ass brains of yours. You'd get entirely too much pleasure out of seeing him suffer for me to even think that you aren't toying with him the same way you're torturing Bre'ana. You're sick and you're an asshole, and that's a bad combination."

"You'd better watch your mother fucking mouth. And for the record, I didn't drag you into anything. Your nosey ass insisted on being a part of it. I didn't need your help. And you're no better than me. I don't see you giving her any free-dom papers either," Tristian scoffed.

I glared at him, offended. 'Freedom papers'? Had he lost his damned mind? I was nobody's slave. Was that the purpose behind this heavy ass chain he was using to keep me bound? How dare he make a reference like that and think it was okay? My mind was running rampant.

"What the fuck is wrong with you, Tristian? We weren't raised like this. Our parents don't make racial comments and prejudiced remarks. We were never taught or told that that was okay. It's offensive. I can only imagine how Bre'ana feels sitting here listening to you talk like that." Kyle's tone was low and it dripped in disappointment. He looked like he was ready to completely disown his brother.

"I'm not prejudiced. I'm not a racist. I'm not saying any-thing that they don't say themselves. I have nothing against them. Bre'ana is black and I love her."

"'They'? 'Them'? The sad part is that you don't even realize that you just proved my point," Kyle said as he shook his head. "It doesn't matter what they say about or call themselves. That doesn't give you the right to do it. Women call each other bitches all the time, but that doesn't grant a man permission to do it as well. There's a certain level of hurt that accompanies certain terms. There are lines that just shouldn't be crossed. As the younger brother, I shouldn't have to tell you this, but it seems you skipped certain critical life lessons."

"Who the fuck do you think you're talking to, standing there criticizing and correcting me? I'll beat your little maggot ass, Kyle. Don't act like you forgot!" Tristian threatened him.

I just shook my head. The entire show was just sad. Kyle was trying to talk some sense into his brother and Tristian would have done well to listen to him, but his pride and his ego fucked up the lesson Kyle was trying to teach. I was disgusted. My mind was telling me that I should have killed Tristian's ass when I had the chance. I would have done the world a great service by eighty-sixing his ass. At the same time, I had never killed anyone. Tristian could definitely be the first though.

I sat there and listened to them going back and forth as if I wasn't even sitting there. They were giving me an even worse headache than the one I had already been battling. Tristian finally said something about doing something to me, but I missed it because by that point I had tuned them both the fuck out. Tristian came storming over to me much to Kyle's protest. Kyle could see the confusion on my face and kept yelling for Tristian to leave me alone. I pushed Tristian away from me and he stormed off to another room in the house, frustrated. It was obvious whatever he had planned wasn't over. I sat back on the sofa and tried to ready myself for whatever Tristian came back with.

Suddenly, the house was shaken by the front door hitting the floor. Will took one look at Kyle and shot him square between the eyes. His body hit the floor with a thud and Will ran straight over to me. The mixture of emotions was just too much for me. I was sad that Will had just killed Kyle, who was bleeding out on the floor but elated to see my man had not given up searching for me.

"The key," I said and pointed frantically at Kyle as Will tugged on the chain wrapped around my waist. The sight of the open sores on my stomach and hips from the chain broke his heart. It was written all over his face. Will looked back at Kyle's corpse, rushed over to him, and searched his pockets. He pulled a key ring out of Kyle's right pocket and brought them over to me.

"Which key is it, baby?" he asked as he fumbled with the ring of keys.

"I- I don't know," I whined as Will began trying keys. "But, baby, Tristian…Tristian's… NO!" I screamed as I looked up to see Tristian standing over Will with a leg from the broken table raised over his head. Will ducked out of the way just in time, spun around, and grabbed Tristian by the waist, knocking him to the floor. They straight jacked it out as they rolled around on the floor.

Will had dropped the keys just out of my reach, and his gun had landed just beyond that. I held an end of my blanket in both hands and scooped the set of keys to myself. I frantically tried key after key on the ring of what must've been thirty or more keys, my fingers shaking as I tried to hurry, knowing that the fight would boil down to whoever got to that gun first. Constantly glancing back and forth between the keys and the pile of tangled arms and flying fists, I fell into a panic trying to find the key to unlock my chain.

Tristian ducked and dodged a blow from Will and grabbed the table leg he had swung at Will at the beginning of the fight. Will spun around and caught the table leg with his face, falling to the floor unconscious. The lock snapped as Will's body hit the floor. I gasped and looked up at Tristian who saw what had just happened in my lap. In a split second, I lunged for the gun, landing on top of it. Tristian landed on top of me and tried to get the gun from beneath me, but I refused to let him.

I elbowed him in his stomach as he grabbed a handful of my hair and snatched my head back. He buckled with the pain and I aimed my elbow higher, landing a blow to his nose. He growled in pain, but that one second was enough to get him off of me. I grabbed the gun and rose to my feet, but Tristian ran up behind me and threw his arm around my neck, trying to choke me out.

"Will!" I yelled, trying to wake my unconscious boyfriend. "Will, baby get up! Help!" But it was no use. He was knocked out cold. I steadied myself on my feet, closed my eyes and felt Tristian's weight behind me, and then kicked my right leg up as hard as I could behind me, kicking him in the groin just as my strength faltered a bit and I dropped the gun.

Tristian, who was bent over holding his bruised jewels, screamed again. He looked at me with murder in his eyes, released a deep growl, and then ran at me as I was backing up. My foot hit something. In a split second, I looked down at the waste bucket, back up at Tristian, and then back down at the bucket. When Tristian was just close enough, I grabbed the bucket and threw all of its contents directly in his face. Shocked and disgusted, he stopped in his tracks, and I made a mad rush for the gun. Will was rolling over on the floor and looked up just in time to see me standing there with perfect posture, aiming the gun at Tristian's head.

"You bitch!" Tristian yelled, still wiping his eyes.

"My name is Bre'ana," I corrected him, "but you can call me Bacardi Barbie. Yes, I like Bacardi and I twerk on the bar, but I'm not, nor will I ever be, your bitch, trick."

POW! Stomach. POW! Dick. POW! Face shot.

Tristian's body hit the floor. I dropped the gun and ran over to Will.

"Will, baby! Are you okay? Can you see me?"

"Yeah, I'm fine. I can see you," he said as he rubbed his head and stood up. "I'm just glad that you're okay."

"Oh, baby. I thought you'd never find me," I whined.

"I had started to wonder myself," he said, "but I wasn't

giving up. I'd never give up on you, on us."

I could tell he was sincere. He leaned in to kiss me, but I pulled back, causing him to frown up at me.

"I...baby, I stink. As bad as I want to kiss you, hug you, jump all over you, I need a bath and a toothbrush bad," I admitted, and Will laughed at my response.

"My Barbie doll," he sighed. "You don't always have to be so perfect. On your worst day, you look better than all of those bitches on their best day."

"Oh, whatever, Will," I giggled and blushed as I waved him off.

"I'm serious," he said as he lifted my chin and our eyes met. "If there were nine thousand nine hundred ninety-nine stars in the sky, you'd be that ten thousandth star taking over the entire night and out-glowing all of the others. You're not just my whole world, Bre. You're my whole universe. You're the sun, the moon, every star, and every planet in it. I'll take you any way that I can get you, as long as I have you."

"Will, baby, I believe you. I really do. All of that sounds nice and all, but can we go? Like seriously. The mushy, sentimental hero's proclamation for his lady love sounds really great and it's highly appropriate given the circumstances, but honestly, I just want to get the fuck out of here. We've got two dead mother fuckers bleeding out on the floor and a bucket of shit and piss thrown everywhere. I don't even know how long I've been here anymore. I just know I don't want to spend another mother fucking minute in this raggedy bitch,"

I told him. He busted out laughing at me and threw his arm over my shoulder.

"C'mon, Barbie doll. Let's go."

Chapter 24

The ride to the hotel was spent in a deafening, echoing, bellowing silence. Neither of us wanted to listen to the radio and neither of us wanted to talk. Being in each other's company was a whole different level of comforting at that moment. We didn't need anything else. We had each other. Again. Finally.

When we pulled up to the hotel, Will grabbed one of his hooded jackets from the backseat and handed it to me.

"I know how self-conscious you are and I know you never go outside without being on point, so you can use my jacket to cover up so no one sees you," he told me. I threw on the jacket with the hood over my head and followed Will into the hotel and onto the elevator. I stood in the opposite corner of the elevator from him and kept my head down as he pushed the button.

Will was still silent as the elevator began to rise. I looked up to see him staring at me, but I couldn't read the expression on his face. When the elevator stopped, I followed him down the hall and into his room.

"I know you want to take a bath and everything," he told me. "I packed you a bag. You've got clothes, shower gel, deodorant, pretty much everything you need," he said as he handed me the duffel bag. "I can leave if you want me to so that you can have the room to yourself."

"I've spent enough time alone. I'd really like you to stay. Please," I said quietly. The reality of the situation was finally sinking in.

"Of course. Whatever you want," he assured me. I watched him sit on the edge of the bed and pick up the remote. "I'll be right here."

Will's suite was beautiful. I walked into the bathroom and was absolutely amazed at how spacious it was. My hand released the duffel bag over the countertop and I went straight to the tub to run myself a bath, but then decided to take a quick shower first so that I didn't end up soaking in a tub of my own soil.

With the shower running, I quickly removed all of my clothes and threw them one by one out of the bathroom door into a pile against the wall. Will brought a plastic bag to the doorway and began tossing the clothes into it. When he looked up at me standing there in my nakedness, he froze in place. I watched as he stood up and tears formed in his eyes. I was confused. Why was he crying?

"Bre'ana, come here," he whispered. I walked over to him and he walked me backwards across the room. When he turned me around to face the full-length mirror, I burst into tears too. "Ssshhh, baby," Will whispered as he stood with his chest against my back. "It's going to be okay."

Until that moment, I had no idea what I looked like. Seeing my own battered and bruised body hurt my heart. My left eye was black and my right jaw was still incredibly swollen. The wounds on my midriff went all the way around my body and they were red, swollen, and infected. I was unusually thin and there were dark circles around my eyes, and bruises up and down both of my arms and legs. I almost didn't even recognize myself.

Looking over my shoulder at Will's reflection, I looked into his crying eyes and realized what that expression had been in the elevator. It was pain mixed with anger. It hurt him to see me in such condition.

"Oh, Will!" I sobbed. "Look at me!"

"Ssshhh. I know, I know, baby. It's going to be okay. Everything is going to be just fine," he whispered to me. "You're still beautiful, and you always will be."

I turned around and sobbed into his chest as he wrapped his arms around me. I couldn't believe how mutilated I looked. And what was worse was that Tristian- a man I had known and trusted all of my life- had done this and so much more to me.

"Go ahead and clean yourself up, baby girl. I'm going to order some room service so you can eat when you're finished."

I nodded and went into the bathroom, leaving the door open as I got into the shower. I must've scrubbed everything twice and I washed my ass at least four times. There was no such thing as too clean, but I was trying to get as close to it as I could. I shampooed my hair twice and even combed the shampoo through my hair. I did the same with the conditioner and then washed my entire body once more before stepping out of the shower and running myself a bath.

I stood in the mirror and wrapped my hair up in a towel as the hot water filled the tub and created bubbles. I looked a bit better already just from the shower, but I knew the bath would do me even more good.

Will was watching TV and making calls. I couldn't tell who he was talking to, but I counted at least seven phone calls announcing that he had found me and I was with him and two calls issuing out the order. I could tell when he called Lil Nard and A-town, though, because the two of them were just like Will: TTG: Trained to Go. They were ready to do whatever needed to be done and had to be assured and reassured that Tristian was dead.

I soaked in the tub for almost an hour and enjoyed the feeling of not being filthy. Will came and sat next to the tub as I lay there with my eyes closed pretending to be asleep.

"I know you're not sleeping," he chuckled. "I don't want to interrupt your bath, but the food has been here for fifteen or twenty minutes and I don't want it to get cold before you get a chance to eat. I know you must be hungry. You look like they've been starving you."

"They really were," I admitted.

"Well, I ordered you a big bowl of potato soup and a chef salad. I didn't want to over-do it. I figured if you hadn't eaten in a while, putting too much on your stomach at one time would do more harm than good. But once you eat that, we can order whatever you want when you get hungry again. Just pace yourself."

"I understand and I agree. I'll go ahead and eat. I'm tired anyway. I haven't had any decent sleep in what seems like forever. It'll be nice to sleep under you again," I said and then looked up into his eyes. He didn't have to tell me he felt the same way. His eyes said it all. He looked relieved at just the thought.

I rose from the water in unashamed nakedness in front of the man I loved. He helped me dry off and then wrapped me in the soft cashmere robe the hotel had provided. I felt brand new as I sat on the bed and poured Balsamic vinaigrette dressing on my salad.

"Tomorrow," he told me, "we're going to make a couple of stops and then head back home. The sooner we can get settled back in, the sooner we can try to get back to normal."

"That's fine with me," I agreed as I ate. Will told me about what he had been through since I had been kidnapped. I couldn't figure out how he had managed to maintain his sanity throughout the ordeal.

When I finished eating, I sat back against the pillows I had propped against the headboard and watched TV while Will was sitting at the desk with his face in his laptop.

"Bang," I heard him say, "I'm coming through there tomorrow before I head home. Can you find the guy you had over there the last time? I want to thank him for his help."

When he got out of the shower, he climbed into the bed with me, wrapped himself around me, and the two of us got the best sleep we had had in months.

*   ~   *   ~   *

Of course, we slept later than we intended. It was afternoon when we woke up, but it didn't matter. We weren't on a schedule. We got dressed and checked out of the hotel. I had Will take me by both of my parents' offices so that they could see me in person without being able to make a huge fuss over me.

"Where else do we need to go before we leave?" I asked Will as we left my father's office.

"To my guy Big Bang's house. Him and his brother Goose helped me quite a bit," Will said as he made a left onto the interstate entrance ramp.

Pulling into the driveway of the house, Will got out and opened my door.

"C'mon," he said. "They'll be happy to meet you."

The moment Will turned to face the house I knew something was up. His facial expression, his gait, his entire demeanor changed. When he opened the front door and marched inside, I hesitated to follow.

"Bre, come in and close the door," Will instructed. "First, I'd like you to meet Big Bang and Goose. This is Bre'ana," he introduced us. The atmosphere suddenly felt serious and rushed. The three of us waved at each other cordially and then Will told them to step aside. I gasped in horror.

"What is this?" I looked back and forth between the three of them. "What's going on?"

"Do you recognize this man, Bre'ana?" Will asked me.

"Yes... well... what's left of him."

"Where do you know him from?" Will demanded.

"He...ummm...well, he..."

"Okay! Okay! Shit! Yes! I did it! I kidnapped her!" the guy interrupted. Goose punched him in his already beaten and bloody face.

"Who the fuck are you?" I whined.

"Tristian is my nephew. He knew that you'd run and probably shoot if you saw him approaching you, especially in Georgia, so he got in touch with me to ask me about my father's old house. When he told me what he was planning to do, I told him I'd help him," the man hurriedly explained.

"Tell her why he would even call you about this shit while you're at it," Will demanded. "Tell her why you're homeless and sleeping in your truck and in that old ass house in the middle of nowhere. Tell her about the kidnappings, rapes, and murders you were charged with and got away with because of a fucking technicality. Tell her how you're an expert at this shit and you knew exactly how to get your hands on the chloroform. You're homeless because you can't get a job because all of this shit is still on your record and most reputable companies don't want to hire someone who is a known kidnapper, molester, and murderer! Did he touch you, Bre? Did any of them touch you?" he roared in anger.

"No! He didn't touch me. I mean, Tristian, he tried. He tried to rape me almost every day, but I kept fighting him off," I told him, still in shock.

"So you came over here high, mumbling to Bang and Goose about screams you were hearing, but all the while you knew exactly who it was and where it was coming from. And when Goose found you and brought you here so you could re-tell the story, you were sober and covered up everything you knew," Will growled as he approached the man. "Not only are you sick in the head, but you condoned and assisted your nephew in the sick ass shit he was doing. You were hearing screaming because you were right outside of the house. And you thought a mother fucker wouldn't put that shit together. I put that shit together, bitch!" Will punched the guy in his face and even though I cringed as the blood splattered across the wall, I enjoyed it. "You owe my girl an apology," Will huffed. "Apologize to her."

"I'm...I'm sorry," he whimpered.

"That's not good enough. She can't hear you," Will said.

"I'm sorry for kidnapping you. I'm sorry," he cried. He was obviously in pain. I didn't care.

"Then you're complaining about hearing her crying and

screaming? How about I make it so you don't have to worry about that? Huh?" Will said and then forced the man's head to the side and punched him repeatedly directly in his left ear as he screamed until crimson red blood began to run from his ear. I covered my mouth with both of my hands to prevent my gasps and whines from escaping as the beating continued. "Do you see her face? Look at her face!" he yelled in the man's right ear. "She has black eyes, a swollen jaw, and a busted lip! And that's just what's left of it. There's no telling what's been done to her that has already healed! And you were complaining about hearing her screaming? Hearing her crying in the middle of the night? She was screaming because she was being beaten and tortured. She was crying because she wanted to go home. She was crying for me! But that's okay because you'll never hear another woman scream or any other sound ever again. I hope you remember what the birds sound like when then sun first shines over the tops of the trees in the morning. I hope you remember what raindrops sound like against a windowpane and what a child's laughter sounds like echoing in a school hallway. I hope you remember what bacon sounds like when it sizzles in the frying pan, what hot water sounds like when you run a bath, what the air conditioner sounds like when it turns on, what a car sounds like when it cranks, and what a car construction sit sounds like when everyone is at work because believe me, your memories are all you're going to have to work with from now on." He then forced the man's head in the opposite direction and slapped his ear repeatedly with an open had until that one bled as well and the man was crying out in unbearable agony.

I touched the swollen side of my face with my fingertips, suddenly self-conscious. Though I had begun to heal, I knew it still looked bad and probably would for a long time. I had told myself in the mirror that morning that even when the knots, swelling, and bruises went away, the blood clot in my right eyeball would still be there for a few additional weeks as a reminder of what I had just endured, and the wounds on my stomach and sides would likely leave scars that may eventually fade, but they'll never go away.

Both eardrums busted and now deaf to the world, the man teeter-tottered side to side in the chair, his equilibrium completely gone. Nothing in me would allow me to feel sorry for him. He had heard my cries in the middle of the night and left me there. He himself had done the same thing to women in his past. He deserved to die.

I looked at Goose and Big Bang and noticed how unbothered they appeared to be. I wondered if this was the norm for them if they assaulted people all the time. Goose definitely looked like he worked out a bit both in the gym and on a nigga's face.

"C'mon, Roadie," Big Bang said, calling Will by the term he used with his closest friends. "Put the mane out of his misery. I ain't for the playing and shit today."

'Today'? Did Will usually beat niggas' asses at their house?

"What you thinking, Barbie doll?" Will asked me. "Should I beat his ass to death or shoot him?"

"Nah," I shook my head. "Beat his ass, throw him in the truck, and dump him with his nephews out in Fayette County. We can chain his ass up the same way they did me and leave him there."

"Sounds good, but I'm not going back out there and I don't suggest you go out there either. How about we beat his ass, toss him in the back of the truck, and then dump his ass in the trees on the side of the road on the way home?" Will suggested.

"That's cool. Break his legs so he can't walk off and make sure he's knocked the fuck out at the end so he feels all the pain," I told them.

"Wow, she's a natural," Goose mumbled.

"Cool. And when we're finished, we'll go get your truck so you can head home. I'll handle the rest of this."

"No, we'll stick together. That way we both have an alibi. Two heads are better than one."

"Aight. Cool," Will nodded. "Whatever you want. You gone stay and watch?"

"Yep," I said as I plopped down in a chair to watch the show.

Will and Goose commenced to beating Tristian's uncle's ass while I sat and watched and Big Bang retrieved a two by four from a back room. Blow after blow, the man was crying and hollering and I was unmoved. He was punched in the eyes so many times they were swollen to the size of golf balls and completely closed. Blood was all across the walls and floor. He had peed on himself twice and his urine was pooled underneath the chair. Three of his teeth were lying on the floor and his mouth was pouring blood. When he lost consciousness, Will kicked the chair from underneath him and they beat him until he woke back up. Will talked shit to him even though he knew he couldn't hear him, and then punched him over and over as his head bounced off the floor.

I couldn't understand why he wasn't dead, but he was barely clinging to life. Will looked at his own knuckles which must have been killing him because three of them were split open.

"Go pop the trunk, Barbie doll, and get in the car," he instructed me. I did as I was told.

A few minutes later, Will, Big Bang, and Goose came out of the house carrying the man. His legs were obviously broken in several places and he was utterly unrecognizable. He looked more like a bloody mass than an actual human being.

Some kind of way, I still had to be myself. I jumped out of the truck and hugged both Goose and Big Bang and thanked them. Of course, they wanted to hear nothing of it, feeling undeserving of my gratitude, but I offered it all the same. I got back into the truck with Will chuckling and shaking his head at me, and we pulled off.

We pulled up to Tristian's house and Will pulled my keys out of his pants pocket.

"Got these from your friend before we left," he said as he

handed them to me.

"Thank you, baby," I beamed.

"Meet me at the gas station by the hospital so we can gas up and then we'll hit the road," he instructed. "It's going to be a long drive."